The truth was all
she wanted from him

"Look," grated Adam, "if you want me to give it to you straight, sure, I did hope to have a shot at getting you to change your mind about selling the place—who wouldn't in my position? A friendly discussion, what's wrong with that?"

"Nothing," she shot back, "only you didn't say a word to me about it. Were you waiting until we...got to know each other better. Was that it?"

His eyes were ice-cold. "Something like that."

She threw him an accusing look. "If only you'd told me—"

"A bit of trust in me might help!" The words seemed to cost him an effort. But how could she ever trust him again? Had their lovemaking meant nothing to him?

Books by Gloria Bevan

HARLEQUIN ROMANCES

These books may be available at your local bookseller.

For a free catalog listing all titles currently available,
send your name and address to:

Harlequin Reader Service
P.O. Box 52040, Phoenix AZ 85072-2040
Canadian address: Stratford, Ontario N5A 6W2

Greek Island Magic

Gloria Bevan

Harlequin Books

TORONTO • NEW YORK • LONDON
AMSTERDAM • PARIS • SYDNEY • HAMBURG
STOCKHOLM • ATHENS • TOKYO • MILAN

Original hardcover edition published in 1983
by Mills & Boon Limited

ISBN 0-373-02618-8

Harlequin Romance first edition May 1984

CHAPTER ONE

'So you're Elizabeth Kay, the girl from New Zealand?' the Greek lawyer said in his excellent English, and motioned her to a seat opposite him at the wide office desk.

'That's me!' She smiled cheerfully and dropped down to a low chair. 'Only no one ever calls me anything but Liz. I couldn't *wait* to get here!' she ran on in her eager husky voice. 'I booked a seat on the first plane leaving for Athens after I got your letter telling me about—' the excitement in her eyes clouded over, 'about my uncle having died and leaving me his property in Crete.'

'Quite, quite. Naturally you will wish to see the place . . .' His voice trailed into silence as he took in his client, a slim girl with a cloud of dark curly hair springing away from a golden-tanned forehead, a sweetly curved mouth and those huge grey-blue eyes. All at once his expression changed to warm intimacy, and Liz was acutely aware of his interest in her as a woman. How could she help it? There was no mistaking the unspoken significance of his look. She could feel his eyes raking her, mentally stripping her, but she willed herself to an attitude of cool detachment and said with what she hoped was an air of nonchalance, 'You knew my uncle? I guess you must have done, seeing that you attended to his legal affairs.'

The warm expression in his dark eyes lingered, but at least, Liz thought with relief, his tone was perfectly controlled.

'For many years. Although I didn't see him often. He visited me only when he had affairs that must be attended to, like drawing up a new will. A fairly straightforward one in this case, there seem to be no complications.' Wrenching his glance away from Liz's face, he rose to take a file from a shelf above his head and seating himself once

again, ran his gaze over the typed paper in his hand.
'Under the terms of the will, the Villa Athene and the
beach taverna are to be shared equally between you and
your uncle's stepdaughter, Katina, who I understand is
continuing to live at the villa. She is a Greek girl of about
your own age,' another warmly intimate glance which Liz
countered with a blank expression, 'not a blood relative, of
course. It seems that your uncle married a Greek woman,
a widow with one child. Unfortunately the wife died soon
after the marriage and the girl was brought up by relatives
in the country. When she was old enough to earn her
living she came to help her stepfather in the taverna on the
beach. In the circumstances I would have thought—' He
broke off. 'However, that was your uncle's decision. There
was a small legacy also, sufficient, your uncle told me at
the time he made the will, for you to make a trip out to
Greece. You have already received the cheque for the
amount?'

'Oh yes,' Liz assured him in her breathless way. 'That
was wonderful of him, to make it possible for me to come
here! There was enough money for the return fare,' she
confided, 'but I'm not worrying about that.' A throaty
laugh had the effect of evoking an even warmer glance
from the swarthy-looking man seated opposite her. 'I just
wanted to get out here and stay.'

He didn't seem to share her enthusiasm. 'You do
realise—' He was back to his legal approach, Liz thought
with relief, 'that sale of the property would require the
consent of both you and your—'

'Cousin?' Liz put in helpfully. 'She's near enough to
being my cousin, and I've always thought of her that way.'
But he seemed anxious only to get his point across to her,
and after all, the thought flashed through Liz's mind,
anything was preferable to the amorous expression on the
dark face. Such a foreign-looking face, she mused, that big
beaky nose and thick, thick black hair. He looked far too
plump for a young man, but maybe that was the effect of
the olive oil that featured so highly in Greek cooking. She

brought her wandering thoughts back to the smooth tones. 'I have Katina's assurance that she is most anxious to dispose of the property. With her no doubt it is a matter of obtaining money for her dowry.'

'A dowry?' Liz stared at him in disbelief. 'Really? These days?'

He smiled at her expression of astonishment. 'It is the custom in our country, when marriage is being discussed by the parents of the two young people, that the girl brings a dowry to the union. The man provides the land, the home, the furnishings.'

Liz was thinking that the subject was bringing back the smouldering warmth to his eyes and in an effort to change the conversation she said briskly, 'Well, I don't see how that affects me one way or the other.'

'Oh, but there you are mistaken! I assure you that it does! Without your agreement to sell your share of the property the whole estate is tied up and nothing can be done.' All at once his tone was dominating and definite. 'I must point out that it would be to your advantage to meet your—er—cousin, as you term her, in this matter. Especially in view of the fact,' he leaned back in his swivel chair regarding her with appreciative melting dark eyes, 'as I have already received an offer to sell on your and Katina's behalf, a most generous offer when one considers the general state of disrepair of the villa and the isolation of the area.' Liz felt there was something mesmeric in his fixed brown stare. 'My client is at the moment most eager to purchase and I would strongly advise you to take advantage of the offer.'

'But—'

He raised a hand to brush aside her objections and swept on. 'Actually the property is situated in a remote area along the coast and wouldn't attract buyers as a general rule, but my client happens to be the owner of one of the luxury hotels built not far away—one moment, I will tell you his name—'

'Don't trouble,' she cut in, 'I'm not interested one little

bit!' She flashed him a brilliant smile. 'So what does it matter who he is?'

The lawyer took not the slightest notice of her words. Clearly he was a man who didn't submit to defeat easily. His smile was tolerant and confident. 'You will change your mind when you see the property. So much repair is needed, so much money would have to be spent on the villa—' He spread out plump hands in an expressive gesture. 'After all, when you live on the other side of the world—'

'Sell my property in Crete? Goodness, no!' Liz stared back at him with wide, incredulous eyes. 'I wouldn't dream of parting with it. I've only just got it!'

He pursed thick red lips. 'We shall see.' At last, Liz thought with relief, she had managed to get her own ideas through to him. She brought her mind back to the lawyer's tones. 'I see you have already made up your mind, but if in the future you should change your mind in the matter, you must let me know. Meantime, I shall tell my client—'

'Tell him anything you like! I don't care, so long as you make it clear to him that there's nothing doing in that direction and if he's counting on me selling out he's wasting his time. Do you know, I've been looking forward to coming to Crete for ages and ages—'

Her companion however was not to be diverted. 'My client is most insistent on purchase, and the price he has offered is far in excess of market value, an opportunity you would be wise to consider before it is too late.'

Liz laughed. 'Too late for what? Not for me!' At his disapproving expression she ran on, 'Don't you see? It's not just a matter of money. It means an awful lot to me, this property of my uncle's. I wouldn't give it up for anything. Not now—or ever!'

'I see.' Liz felt a surge of relief that he appeared convinced that she really meant what she had said. He made no further protest, nor did he advance any more arguments. So why did she get the impression that whatever his appreciation of her physical charms, he put her down as a silly little fool with no business acumen whatever? That when it came to a question of self-interest she registered zero, not even bothering to ascertain the identity of the prospective buyer. As if she cared! Probably he was some Greek business man, so what did it matter? Confidingly she leaned towards him. 'Shall I tell you something? It doesn't seem at all strange to me being here in Crete, even though I come from a country that's so far away.'

'Indeed?' He was eyeing her attentively, as though he had all the time in the world, Liz thought, and banished a niggling suspicion that he was interested in the curves of her mouth rather than in what she was telling him. Dropping her gaze for fear he might read the thoughts that were passing through her mind, she ran on.

'I guess I was attached to Uncle Jim because he was the only relative I had. My parents were drowned in a boating accident when I was a small child, and you can't really count foster-parents, even if they're kind and look after you. But Uncle Jim was different.'

'He corresponded with you?'

'All the time! Even when I was a little girl at school—' Her tone softened. 'He used to send me the funniest letters, the sort with sketches on them and big print that even a seven-year-old could read. He was fifteen years older than my dad. Uncle Jim put his age up a year or two when World War Two broke out. He went away with an N.Z. Army contingent and was sent to Crete. He liked the island so much that after years spent in a prison camp he decided not to return to New Zealand but to make his home in Crete. He bought property there and married a Greek woman he'd got to know in wartime. It was such a pity that she died soon afterwards.' A tender smile played around Liz's soft lips. 'So then he just stayed on at his villa, working at the taverna. He wrote me long letters about his life and I knew I could recognise the Villa Athene right away just from his descriptions of it. He told me all about the taverna on the beach too. He used to work there himself with the help of a Greek couple, a middle-aged man and his wife, and much later, when she was old enough to leave home, Katina came to help too. He served meals at the taverna, Greek food, of course. And the beach—he sent me pictures of it and it looked fabulous. He wrote me that he swam every day in the bay,' her bright expression clouded over, 'until he got ill and had to rest a lot. But he still went on writing to me! I'd been saving up for ages for a trip to Greece. It was something that I'd set my heart on, a surprise visit to my uncle here. You wouldn't believe how hard it was.' Her soft lips twitched at the corners. 'I really had to work at it.' Silently she added, especially when it came to not letting myself get too deeply involved in love affairs. That way I knew I would never get here. She ran on, 'I'd got about half of my air fare money saved when I got your letter. I couldn't believe it at first,' her voice thickened, 'that he wouldn't be here to meet me . . . not ever.' Her eyes misted over. 'Now everything's different. It's such a pity,' she choked on the last word.

'I understand your feelings.' The Greek lawyer leaned forward to place his plump hand over hers and Liz felt the pressure of his moist palm. She swallowed the lump in her throat and recovered her hand. 'So now you know,' she said briskly, 'why I don't want to sell my share of the place that Uncle left me.'

He threw her a thoughtful glance. 'You say you have no capital, only your return fare to New Zealand. It would not be possible for you to find employment at the village. Had it been at Heraklion, now, or Chania—What did you do for a living at home? Nursing? Schoolteaching?'

Liz shook her head. 'I just did office work—typing, keeping accounts, all that stuff.'

He raised his eyes heavenwards. 'If you want my opinion—'

Liz didn't, but she could see he was determined to hand her out advice, so she sighed impatiently and forced herself to listen. 'You have no choice in the matter—none at all. How can you stay here without capital or employment of any sort?'

'Don't worry about me,' Liz said cheerfully. 'I'll find something. So long as I can stay . . .'

To her surprise he was growing red in the face, a dark unbecoming brick colour. With hands gesticulating wildly in the air he shouted, 'Me, I am trying to tell you for your own good and you will not listen!'

There was no doubt, the thoughts ran through her mind, that he was a man who couldn't endure to have his counsel ignored. After all, she conceded, folk came here to ask, and pay, for his advice. But to become so wildly excited over her refusal to take his words seriously . . . it must be the Greek way.

'I just want to live here for a while,' she said in an effort to calm his ruffled feelings. Her throaty laugh rang out. 'Wouldn't it be funny if history repeated itself and I got so wrapped up in the island that I couldn't leave it either, and just stayed on for ever?'

In a lightning change of mood he was smiling, his warm intimate glance lingering on her face before travelling over her slim body. If only he wasn't becoming amorous again!

He smirked. 'Marry a Greek man, maybe?'

Liz laughed, mainly in an effort to dispel his fatuous expression. 'Who's talking about husbands?' In spite of herself she felt a tinge of pink creeping up her cheeks and before he could make something of the innocent remark she said hurriedly the first words that rushed into her head. 'What's wrong with my living at the villa? It can't be all that dilapidated if Katina is still living there. Maybe we could run the taverna together and live at the villa. From what you've told me there's only my Greek cousin living there, and I'm sure there'd be room for both of us.'

All at once he was back to her legal adviser. He regarded her reprovingly. 'You do not understand—so much you do not understand about our country. You should listen to me.'

A shaft of remorse struck her. After all, the man was trying to help her in his own way. If only his way wasn't an amorous one! 'All right, then,' she threw him a smile, 'I'm listening.'

'It will not be suitable for you to live at the Villa Athene.'

His words surprised her and she stared back at him in disbelief.

'Why ever not? There's room for me, isn't there?'

'That is not the problem. Has it not occurred to you that your cousin, as you term her, may not be pleased at sharing her inheritance from her stepfather with a stranger, someone she has never set eyes on? She may well feel resentment towards you, and even more so when she hears that you are not agreeable to parting with the property.' Was he having another dig at her? Liz wondered. 'She could be angry with you, and Greek girls,' he said significantly, 'show their feelings. If I were you—'

'But you're not, are you?' Liz cut in. 'If that's all you're warning me about, my cousin . . .' She couldn't imagine anything going wrong for her on this sundrenched summer day when things were happening and she was on her way to claim her inheritance. She said with a smile, 'Don't worry about it. I'll soon talk her out of it.'

He looked unconvinced. The next moment his gaze dwelt on Liz's alive face, the sort of face, he noted, that mirrored every emotion, and plainly, right at this moment, happiness was there plain to see. 'You have a saying in your country,' he observed smilingly, 'something about not meeting trouble halfway? So that was your only connection with the Greek islands?'

She laughed. 'Not quite. Would you believe? I had a neighbour at home who came from Crete, a nice girl with two little children. Her brother had come out to New Zealand to work in a restaurant in Auckland and he sent for his sister to come over to New Zealand for a holiday. When she decided to make her home there her parents in Crete sent her photographs of three different young men who were interested in a wife. So she didn't have much choice in the matter of picking a husband. Isn't it amazing!'

He looked unimpressed. 'It is the custom in Greece—'

'Yes, I know. The funny thing about it all is,' Liz admitted reluctantly, 'that they're awfully happy and really in love with each other.' She put her head on one side, considering. 'Odd, isn't it?'

'Not at all.' His voice dropped to a low intimate tone. 'A man can want a girl to be his woman. The manner of meeting, it is of no importance.' His eyes said, 'I could feel that way about you.'

To avoid a dangerous moment Liz hurriedly changed the subject, scarcely thinking of what she was saying. 'So of course when Yanni and Angelike knew I was coming here they were ever so excited. They gave me gifts to pass on to their families and loads of photographs of the children. I've been looking at my Crete map and it doesn't seem too far away from where I'll be at my uncle's villa, to take a bus ride up there to see them one day.'

His swarthy plump face was set and resentful, no doubt because of her rejection of his intimate words. If only Greek men weren't subject to swift changes from light-heartedness to rage, even rage that they were trying to conceal. She had had to make it clear to him that she wasn't interested in him, as a man, that was.

She brought her mind back to the words of the man facing her. Sulkily he murmured, 'You should ring for a taxi from the hotel. Meantime,' all at once he was brisk and businesslike once more, 'here are the keys to the villa and taverna,' he handed her a sealed envelope. 'If your stepsister happens to be away from the villa when you arrive, you may need them. I will arrange transport for you on a bus leaving at two this afternoon from the depot outside the old Venetian wall. You must look for the Kolos destination sign.'

'Thanks! That's super!' Liz got to her feet and reached

down to pick up her travel pack, then slipped the straps over her shoulders.

'Ask the driver to put you down at the Hotel Hermes,' he was saying. He rose from the desk and stood facing her, a dark-eyed man of medium height with black curly hair and a prominent nose. 'You must promise me that if you have any problems at all you will call on me for help.'

'Problems?' she echoed bewilderedly. 'Oh, you mean language difficulties and all that?'

'Anything! Anything at all!' His warm glance lent the words significance, or was she merely imagining it? Maybe he really did want to help her and she had misjudged him.

Taking her small hand in a soft clammy clasp, he pressed her fingers to his moist lips. 'If there's any way I can be of service to you, you won't hesitate to let me know? Remember, I will be only as far away from you as the nearest telephone!'

'I'll remember,' said Liz, and recovered her hand. Privately she was of the opinion that she would need to be in desperate straits indeed to throw herself on the mercy of this amorous Greek. Her bright smile, however, gave nothing away.

He ushered her to the door, his gaze lingering on her slim figure as she went along the passage. Well, he congratulated himself, he had done what he could for this attractive-looking girl with the dancing light of excitement in her eyes. With luck he would be seeing her again before long, because once she realised the state of disrepair of her newly acquired property she would change her mind soon enough about getting rid of the old place. He'd take a bet with anyone that she would be back with him in his office within a week.

Liz emerged from the dimness of the office building into the strangely brilliant white light of the Greek islands. The town, she saw, was ringed with hills, blue in the distance. Ahead of her stretched the winding cobbled street with its shops and taverns and below were the thick

Venetian walls and stone archways that had once guarded
the old port. Along the waterfront quaint dark little stores
had muslin dresses and blouses hung in doorways and in
the harbour the cruise liners were bright with coloured
flags and canvas awnings. All at once she was swept by a
sense of heightened perception, born of the dazzling clear
air and her exotic surroundings. It was all just as her uncle
had described it to her in his letters, and now she was
really, really here! If only he were here to welcome her.
She brushed the regretful thoughts away. He would want
her to enjoy her stay in Crete, to fall a victim to its lure just
as he had done. It's true, she told herself in amazement, all
they say in novels and travel brochures about the Aegean
Sea. It really is that unbelievable blue.

She went on up the narrow street past a medieval
church where sanctuary bells were tolling over town and
harbour. Bells are ringing for me too, she mused, and once
again felt that surge of elation. Presently she found herself
merging into the flow of people who were milling around a
stone fountain where water rose high in the air in the
tree-shaded square. Liz made her way through the
crowd—well-dressed tourists with guide books and
cameras, Greek Orthodox priests, bearded men in black
robes and tall black hats, Greek women, their sun-dried
brown faces shaded by dark coifs. She made her way
towards a taverna with its checked red tablecloths,
wooden chairs, small tables and blue canopies. The out-
door eating place was crowded and as she made her way
towards a secluded corner, Liz tried to ignore the obvious
interest of swarthy men seated at the main cluster of
tables.

As she waited for a waiter to take her order, her gaze
drifted over the chattering crowd around her. So many
Greek men, and all so volatile. Did they not take their
wives or girl-friends for coffee? she wondered. Suddenly
her gaze was arrested by a party of Greeks at a nearby
table where the men were wildly gesticulating and shouting, obviously engaged in an argument of such passionate

intensity that she expected a fist fight to flare up at any moment. The next moment she saw to her surprise that the men were now smiling and chatting with one another, apparently the best of friends. Unfortunately they were eyeing her with bright interested glances and Liz promptly averted her eyes from the exuberant group, telling herself that it was her own interest in the party that had evoked the spate of Greek comments, clearly concerning erself, that were echoing around the table. She was ginning to realise that as a stranger in a foreign country, avelling alone, she must learn to cope with the Greek nale's uninhibited interest. If only she knew the language of the country—but the trip had come about without warning and there had been no time for her to do more than buy a small language travel guide of basic phrases, and what use was that, she asked herself, when what was needed for a girl travelling solo was some instruction on how to say 'Get lost!' or 'I'm waiting for my husband!'

She lingered over the thick Greek coffee, enjoying the brilliant sunshine, fascinated by the variety of accents echoing around her—Canadian, English, American, even the Australian 'twang'.

Time fled by and almost before she realised it, a glance at her wrist watch told her it was time to adjust the shoulder straps of her nylon pack and make her way to the depot to board the bus for the small village along the coast that was her destination.

The Greek driver recognised the name of the village at once when she enquired of him, but she had no idea whether her efforts to make him understand that she wished to be put off at the hotel stop when they arrived there registered with him. She would just have to hope that he did, she told herself, and took her seat next to an elderly Greek woman, whose nut-brown face was wrinkled from the hot summer suns of the island.

Except for herself, she noticed, the passengers were all Greeks who were talking and laughing amongst themselves. Liz stared out of the window as the vehicle moved away, taking in the jumble of little streets with their small dimly lighted stores, where shopkeepers stood in door-ways amongst the beads and bells and muslin embroid-ered dresses fluttering in the breeze. Presently they left the town behind, taking a quiet highway where wild flowers, blood-red poppies and white daisies, lined the roadsides, and mountains were clear cut against a translucent blue sky. They were out of sight of the sea now, climbing high hills sparsely covered with silvery green olive trees and fragrant with the scent of herbs, rosemary and thyme. After a time they swung into a road running along the sea coast and Liz eagerly took in the passing scenes—blue bays where tavernas were built at the water's edge, stark white stone houses clinging to steep dry hill-sides. She craned her neck backwards to watch a young Greek boy riding a donkey ambling down a rocky slope.

It was a long drive, longer than she had expected, and the white heat of the day was fading when at last the bus turned a bend and ran down towards a rocky coast where waves dashed against dark cliffs and the only building in sight was an opulent hotel, a luxuriously appointed mod-ern building with an imposing facade and great glass windows facing the sea. Liz wondered why the driver was drawing up here as no one seemed to be moving, then all at once she realised he was eyeing her enquiringly. The next moment he burst into a flood of Greek. At last she managed to pick up a word, Kolos. But that was her destination. There must be some mistake. The thoughts rushed confusedly through her mind—there was no vil-lage anywhere in sight, no houses, nothing but this im-mense impressive hotel.

Helplessly she appealed to the driver, gesticulating, appealing to him in her own language, but his answering spate of Greek did nothing to reassure her. At last, to her relief, a passenger rose from his seat at the back of the vehicle and came to join them. He was a Greek, by his accent, she realised, middle-aged and friendly, and thank heaven, he spoke English. Rapidly he translated the excitable Greek words into her own language. 'I know it's Kolos,' she replied distractedly, 'but I want to go to the Villa Athene! It's near a beach and there's a taverna there too. I can't understand it—the name is the same, unless there are two places named Kolos—please will you tell him?'

Swiftly he translated the message and a rapid interchange of words ensued, then the stranger turned to her with a reassuring smile. 'He says you are to get out here. It is not far to the next bay. You must follow the goat track through the olive trees over the hill,' he gestured to a dry slope, 'and there you will find the Villa Athene.'

'Oh, *thank* you!' Her wide smile included her benefactor as well as the Greek driver. Suddenly everyone was happy, the sun-wrinkled face of the Greek woman at her side broke into a beaming smile and the passengers talked, waved and gesticulated with what Liz took to be friendly good wishes towards her. Then she found herself out on the white dust of the road. She hesitated, her gaze taking in the opulent hotel that appeared so bright and welcoming. Could it be the masses of green growing plants cascading over stark white walls, or maybe the pink geraniums spilling from great urns at the entrance, that made it seem so attractive to her travel-weary senses?

'Come to think of it,' she told herself, 'I'm not sure whether or not there'll be anyone at the villa, not really. There could be no food there, nothing to drink. I've only got vague directions as to how to find the place,' she reasoned. 'I'm not sure if I'll be able to recognise it, especially as it will soon be dark.'

Liar. A tiny voice of truth piped deep in her mind. You're feeling awfully weary all of a sudden and not in a mood for a confrontation with that Greek sort-of-cousin of yours.

The uneasy thoughts flickered through her mind. Who said anything about a confrontation?

That Greek lawyer with the unpronounceable name, that's who! Well, he hinted as much.

But I thought, jeered the voice, that you were going to talk Katina out of any mistaken ideas she might have about you?

I will! I will! Tomorrow. In the morning I'll be feeling fresher, more able to cope with whatever turns up. After all, came the sneaky thought, what difference could a few hours make? It would be sheer joy to stay just for the night in this luxurious hotel, to revel in a warm shower, eat a meal already prepared and be certain of somewhere to spend the night. Why not? The battle was won.

Liz went through the iron gates and into a spacious foyer. At the reception desk a smiling Greek girl with friendly dark eyes arranged a night's stay for Liz, handed her a room key and then a porter escorted her into a lift that shot them up to a carpeted corridor. The room into which Liz was shown was a delight, she thought. She threw her nylon pack on to the linen bedcover and explored the balcony, the spacious bedroom, the luxuriously fitted bathroom with its blue and white tiled flooring. How could she help but enjoy herself during her brief stay in these unfamiliar, if expensive, surroundings?

The shower, she found, was all she had hoped for, with thick and thirsty towels and delicately perfumed soap. Afterwards she brushed her damp hair until it sprang back in natural waves and curled around her face. Leaving her complexion clear, she made up her eyes with shadow and slipped into a dress she had hesitated about buying, back home in New Zealand. At least she had hesitated about paying the price, but now, glancing in the mirror, she decided that the garment had been well worth it. The soft cotton in a misty shade of lilac set off her dark hair to advantage and did something for her glowing skin. As she met her mirrored reflection she couldn't help the thought that it was too bad there was no one to notice—no one special, that was—someone masculine, of course. To be here alone in Greece . . . it seemed a pity. And yet, she mused, the Greek Islands were the home of pagan gods, of myth and legend, and maybe, who knows, the ancient magic still worked! She flashed a wink in the direction of the mirror girl. *He*, that special someone, could be waiting for her in Crete. Maybe he was right here in the hotel at this moment. And maybe, she pulled a face at her reflection, he wasn't! She turned away and soon she was stepping down the great marble stairway and entering the vast dining room that seemed, at first glance, to stretch away for ever.

A Greek waiter showed Liz to a corner table where long windows reflected a dark sea. Picking up the menu he handed her, she ran her eyes down the items without comprehending their meaning. She smiled up at the waiter at her side. '*Karpousi?* Now what—'

'Iced melon, madam.'

'That'll do me for starters.' Once again she consulted the menu. 'Oh, here's something I'd like to try, squid with salad.'

As the waiter took her order any doubts she had entertained about difficulty in ordering food at the hotel faded away. Why, it was easy? Especially as one dessert, crème caramel, was a familiar name. The meal proved to be delicious. So much so that she boldly ordered a bottle of the native wine, retsina—but one sip of the strong liquid was sufficient to make her push her glass aside, for the wine had to her a strong flavour of—could it be turpentine?

Afterwards she moved into the spacious lounge room, dropping down to a low couch at the side of an attractive-looking woman of middle age. 'I'm Mary Denton,' the stranger had a pleasant easy manner of speaking, 'all the way from Winnipeg. Are you travelling alone through the Greek Islands too?'

'Not any further.' Liz zmiled. 'I'm Liz, all the way from New Zealand. Shall we have coffee together?'

'Love to.' Presently they were sipping strong dark Greek coffee from pottery mugs. 'I'm on a world trip,' the Canadian woman told Liz. 'and I'm looking up my family on the way. I've a son in Mexico and a married daughter living in Australia. But Greece is the country I love most of all,' she confided. 'I've been teaching my college students Greek history for years and I never tire of it. It's the one country I never want to leave although,' she smiled wryly, 'there's just one thing I'd like to see here, and that is tavernas especially for tourists and overseas travellers where one could drop in for coffee and a toasted roll with fillings like we have back home. You know? If there are any such eating places around the Greek Islands, I haven't come across them. I know if I had money to invest in this country I'd put it into building a taverna for tourists, and I'm sure it would be worthwhile. Listen—' On the other side of the wide room Greek musicians were playing bouzoukis, and as the plaintive melody drifted through the room, a group of swarthy looking men wearing mulberry-coloured cummerbunds of their native Cretan style, joined together with arms thrown around their partner's shoulders, as their feet performed the intricate steps.

When the dance was over the two women crossed the room to wander down some steps towards small shops with their attractive window displays of fashion garments with a Greek influence, miniature urns and gold necklaces. 'This place must be going to my head,' Liz told her companion ruefully, holding against her slim waist an exquisitely cut black skirt, its full folds bordered with a traditional design in heavy gold.

'Go on, take it!' Mary Denton encouraged her. 'If you don't you'll be sorry! I'll tell you something—if I were your age and a garment did that much for me I'd skip dinner for a week to pay for it!'

Laughing Liz shrugged her shoulders. 'You have a bad influence on me! All the same—' She threw caution to the winds and made the purchase. 'Though heaven only knows,' she confided to her new-made acquaintance, 'where I'll ever go to wear a garment like this!'

'Don't be too sure,' the older woman told her with a smile. 'Don't forget you're in Greece now, where anything can happen! The thing is to be prepared for it, and then one of these days or nights, you'll be glad you bought that Grecian skirt, you'll see!'

'I only hope you're right.' Already Liz was having second thoughts about the amount of money she had spent, and this was only the start of her stay.

Back in the immense lounge room, however, she soon forgot her qualms, for dance music was pulsing from a stereo and partners appeared at her side as if from nowhere, attracted by the girl with the expression of excitement lighting her blue-grey eyes. Liz danced with a Swiss tour guide, staying the night with his party on their way to a beach resort further up the coast, then with a middle-aged business man with a quiet smile and a charming manner.

'Who was that?' Mary Denton enquired smilingly as the music drew to a close and Liz was escorted back to her seat by a dark man with a heavy moustache.

'Don't ask me!' Liz was breathless and flushed from exertion and the heat of the night. 'He didn't say one word, maybe he didn't know the language!'

It was much later in the evening when she resisted the attempts of the English business man to persuade her to stay on. 'There'll be dancing here for hours yet,' he told her. But Liz held firmly to her decision, and soon she stepped into a lift and was wafted up to her room.

Somehow, in spite of the comfortable mattress, she found difficulty in getting to sleep. Hour after hour, restlessly she turned over her pillow and flung herself from side to side.

She had been asleep for only a few minutes, it seemed to her, when she was awakened by sounds of masculine singing, shouting and roars of laughter from the floor below. She eyed her little illuminated travel clock. Three o'clock in the morning! It was too bad, she thought crossly, for that noisy party below to keep others awake with their revelry! Just let them go on with their noisy exuberance for another half hour and she would do

something about it! In the end she couldn't wait that
long. Suddenly incensed at the uproar echoing from the
floor below, she sprang from bed and without bothering
with a wrap, flung wide the french windows and went out
on the balcony, determined to put an end to the disturb-
ance.

Moonlight silvered the grounds below, making the
scene almost as bright as day, and as she peered over the
railings she saw it was just as she had thought. A noisy
party of Greeks were wandering in and out of a room on
the floor below and out to a balcony directly beneath her.
Clearly they had been imbibing freely, for some of the
group were unsteady in their movements and one of the
party, a swarthy man with a black moustache, caught
sight of Liz and waved a bottle of retsina in the air.

'The noise!' she called down to him. 'Stop the noise! It's
terrible! I can't sleep with that racket going on down
there!'

The next moment she realised to her chagrin that her
angry outburst had had the effect of bringing others out on
to the balcony below. They clustered around the railing,
laughing loudly and brandishing bottles of wine in her
direction. Clearly they were happily unaware of what she
was trying to get through to them and were inviting her to
join their party. Oh, she could kill them! She would soon
disillusion them about that being the reason for her being
out here on the balcony at this hour in the morning. 'No!
No!' She glared down at them angrily. At that moment she
caught behind her an ominous sound. The next moment
she realised that the wide plate glass doors opening on to
the balcony had been caught in a gust of the night breeze
and slammed shut. Forgetting the Greek party below, in
sudden panic she ran to the door, wrenching at the heavy
handles—but it was no use, the doors could only now be
opened from the inside.

Scarcely knowing what she was doing, she ran to the
balcony rail. 'Help, somebody! Help!' The cry seemed to
leave her lips without her volition. Her call for help had

the effect of bringing her once more to the unwelcome
attention of the party of men below. They crowded out to
their balcony, calling up to her in a spate of Greek. Panic
shot through her. Suppose the revellers below had got the
mistaken impression that she was inviting them up to her
apartment? Although somewhat the worse for drink, they
appeared a young and athletic lot—and definitely amorous. Were all Greek men unashamedly womanisers? she
wondered. What if they tried to scramble up to her
balcony? The thought was so appalling that she turned
and hurried back into the shadows, her heart beating fast
as if she had been running. Only there was nowhere to run
to! Wildly she glanced around her. There must be someone besides herself in this great building who had heard
the uproar in the night, someone to whom she could
appeal for help.

There was, she realised the next minute, as a man's tall
muscular figure appeared on the adjoining balcony. 'You
little fool!' To think he was actually blaming her for the
noise that had disturbed his slumbers! 'What do you think
you're doing?'

Liz ran to the corner of the railing and leaned towards
him. 'Me?' Her voice emerged as an indignant squeak. 'It's
not *my* fault! It's those Greeks down there on the next
floor! They've been driving me crazy with all the racket
they've been making, and now,' she finished breathlessly,
'they've been making a nuisance of themselves. They're
. . . annoying me!'

At that moment the moon, emerging from behind a
cloud, flooded the scene with silver radiance. She had an
impression of a strong masculine face, all planes and
angles in the fitful gleam of light, of wide shoulders and a
tall lean frame. He was tying the cord of his dark robe
around his waist. 'What can you expect,' the deep vibrant
tones were tinged with contempt, 'when you go flaunting
yourself at Greek men looking like that? They're in a
party mood and out you come in night gear that doesn't
leave much to the imagination. What the hell did you

think their reaction would be?'

A wave of anger surged through her. Of all the horrible, beastly men! Judging by his accent, he was English, but he was just as bad as the Greeks. 'Flaunting myself?' she cried in horrified protest. 'I don't know what you mean! If you're trying to tell me that I've been inviting trouble from them, that I . . .' Her voice died away. Up till this moment she had been too distraught to give a thought to her attire. Now as the soft night breeze stirred the diaphanous folds of the single garment she wore, she realised the revealing transparency of the sea-green nightgown she had bought especially for her trip to Crete. Hurriedly she stepped back into the shadows.

'What else would you call it?' The contemptuous tones stung her. He made to turn away, and panic gripped her. 'Wait! Don't go!' she cried in desperate entreaty. Hateful though he was, he was her only chance of escape. A sudden onslaught of tears threatened and the words came in a rush. 'You don't understand! You've *got* to help me! I'm in a spot! I came out here to tell those noisy Greek guys to quieten down their party so that I could get some sleep and the door slammed shut behind me and now I can't get back to my room!'

'Really?' She could tell by his tone that he didn't believe her. Callous, unfeeling brute!

'Oh, you're just no help at all!' she threw at him. 'Pretending you don't understand, not believing a word of what I'm telling you. I tried to get those Greeks down there to help me. They don't know any English, but *you* do! And all you can do is to stand there and sneer and say things,' her voice dropped to a sibilant whisper, 'that aren't true at all.'

'How was I to know what your problem was?' he enquired with deceptive gentleness. Oh, he was an unfeeling brute, keeping her out here talking when he had no intention of being the slightest help to her. All at once she decided to throw dignity and resentment to the Cretan moon that had caused her so much trouble tonight.

'Look,' she had no choice but to crush down her anger and appeal to him, 'you've just *got* to help me,' her tones were low and tense with emotion. 'If you don't, I don't know what I'm going to do!' In spite of herself her voice cracked. *'Please!'*

'Now if only you'd asked me nicely before.' The maddening injustice of his remark almost sparked her to forget her resolution to hold on to her temper at all costs if she knew what was good for her. If she didn't—the worrying thoughts chased through her mind—she would be forced to spend what was left of the night a prisoner on the balcony, the butt of coarse jokes (even if she didn't understand them she knew they'd be coarse) from the inebriated group below.

The bland tones cut across her thoughts. 'Now if you'd explained it to me before—'

Exasperated, she cried angrily, 'I've told and told you!' In the heat of her feelings she forgot all about using a soft approach for her own advantage. 'And all you do,' she threw at him, 'is go on and on about my looking provocative, and I'm not,' she stumbled, 'I don't . . . Anyway,' she caught herself up and rushed on, almost incoherent with frustration and rage, 'you're insufferable—you just don't care!' Suddenly all hope of obtaining any assistance from him fled. 'You've no intention of helping me!' she cried. 'It's all just a game to you! It amuses you no end to keep me on tenterhooks!'

'Is that the way you think of me?' His soft innocent tone was infuriating to her taut nerves. 'I must have given you the wrong impression. Something to do with that dark hair of yours falling around your shoulders put me off, made me forget what I was saying. You really shouldn't wear those narrow straps if you don't want your shoulders to be seen.'

'Never mind about my shoulders,' Liz said fiercely. She had abandoned her plan of enlisting the assistance of the dark-haired Englishman. He was nothing but a sadistic brute! 'If I could only open my door,' she breathed, 'I wouldn't stay out here arguing with you one more minute—'

'But you can't, can you? Not when it's locked on the inside,' he reminded her with maddening truth. 'Not to worry. No one should ever get all that het up about things here. Greece is a happy place, didn't anyone ever tell you?'

'Are you going to help me get back to my room or aren't you?' she cut in tersely. To her horror the words ended on a sob, and she couldn't go on. Now he would think, blast him, that she was making a play for his pity. Not that it would affect him in the least, he was so cold and uncaring and generally hateful. She blinked away the moisture from her eyes and said thickly, 'Oh, what's the use!'

'You can relax!' All at once the satirical note was gone from his deep tones. 'Your troubles are over. I'm on my way!'

Liz held her breath. She wouldn't put it past him to climb right back to bed and put her out of his mind. A few minutes later, however, her gloomy thoughts were dispelled as a dark tousled head appeared over the adjoining balcony. 'I've just got through to the night porter on the phone and he's on his way up with your key.'

'Oh, that's wonderful!' breathed Liz on a long sigh of relief. 'You managed to make him understand then? You speak Greek?'

Once again the deep resonant tones were tinged with amusement, but now somehow she didn't mind. 'Well enough. Don't worry, you'll be quite safe in Greece—so long as you keep out of the bright moonlight!'

'Oh, you—' The angry words died on her lips, because he had vanished back into his room. For a moment she knew an odd regret. She supposed, she reflected reluctantly, that she owed him some thanks for his help, but really he didn't deserve it, not after the way he had kept her waiting all that time. Anyway, she defended herself, it had *seemed* a long time. The sound of a key turning in the lock was the most welcome sound she had heard in all her life.

Strangely, in the deep silence of a pre-dawn world, she

found that sleep eluded her. With senses alert, she lay back on the pillows, arms crossed behind her head as she went over and over the events of the last half hour. Odd how the image of the man in the shadows of the next balcony stayed with her—the dark planes of the strong face, the broad shoulders, the slightly sardonic tone of his voice. She would be leaving in the morning, so there was little chance of their ever meeting again. She couldn't understand why the thought was depressing. She'd give a lot to see him just once more. Mere curiosity on her part, of course, for no man could really be so devastatingly good-looking, not in the clear Greek sunlight.

CHAPTER TWO

Liz awakened in the morning to dazzling sunshine streaming over her face, and for a moment she blinked in disbelief. What was she doing here in this unfamiliar room that faced a glittering blue sea? Then, as recollection came back in a rush, she dropped her feet to the tiled floor and, crossing the room, opened the glass doors the merest trifle. She wasn't going to be caught that way again, not without being fully dressed! Silence lay all around her and with luck, she mused, the Greek party on the floor below were still sleeping off the effects of their night of revelry. She couldn't bear it if any of them should recognise her in the light of day. Probably they would sleep for hours yet, she comforted herself, and by the time they began to function once again, she would have left the hotel.

If only she could meet her helper once again—the thought came unbidden. She hadn't yet decided whether he was friend or foe, but could she meet him again, just once, she could settle the matter in her own mind. It was odd, she mused as she pulled her nightdress over tousled dark hair and slipped into panties and bra and a dress of cool cotton, how easy it was for her to forget his mockery, the hateful way in which he had taken his time before coming to her rescue. Now all that seemed important was that he had finally solved her problem.

When she entered the dining room only a few tables were occupied—no doubt the tour party had already left to continue their sightseeing, and she could see no tall masculine figure. She knew she would recognise him again at sight despite the shadows of the balcony. What was the matter with her, she scolded herself, that she couldn't seem to get his lean dark face or the ironic tones of his voice out of her mind?

Back in her room she packed away her dress and nightdress in her nylon travel gear, stuffed in her toilet bag, then adjusting the straps over her shoulders, she made her way down the winding staircase. As she settled her account at the reception desk she realised that the girl seated there spoke in English, and Liz decided to check on her destination.

'It is only a short way to the Villa Athene.' The friendly Greek girl rose from her chair to escort Liz out of the wide foyer and into the dazzling sunshine outside. 'If you take the goat track over the hill,' she indicated a narrow path winding over the rise, 'you will see that it is the only dwelling in the bay. You will come back here?'

'Goodness, no!' Liz's tone was laced with excitement and anticipation. 'I'm going to live there!' She flashed an impish smile. 'Don't you think I'm lucky?'

The girl made no answer and Liz imagined there was a puzzled expression in the dark eyes. She thrust the thought aside. As if anything could possibly go wrong with her wonderful new life! Up till now the only thing at all worrying had been last night's episode on the hotel balcony, and that had been entirely due to her own foolishness in allowing herself to be trapped there. An episode that had ended without harm, thanks to the reluctant assistance of the man in the next room. There she went again, thinking of him! He was a stranger, a shadow-man. Why, she didn't even know his name.

She hurried up the dusty white track winding through the silvery green of sparsely growing olive trees, breathing in air that was redolent with a spicy perfume that was new to her. When she reached the top of the rise she paused, gazing down at the small sheltered bay below. In sharp contrast with the rugged rocky coastline from which she had come, here was an expanse of golden sand washed by a translucent blue sea. Her gaze moved to the foot of the hill where on a grassy strip, half obscured by trees and bushes, she glimpsed the whitewashed walls of a stone villa with faded blue shutters and a tiled roof. From the front entrance steps led down to the sand and a short distance farther down the beach was a small dwelling where under the shade of shabby canvas awnings, wooden tables and chairs spilled out on to the sand. Could it be the emptiness of the scene she wondered, that lent the taverna such a desolate air? But of course, she reminded herself, her uncle would have had to close the taverna at the onset of his illness.

All at once she couldn't wait to take a closer look at her inheritance. Her pack bumping on her shoulders, she ran down the curving track, to emerge hot and flushed, amid a screen of tall oleander bushes with their clouds of pink blossoms. Liz, however, had eyes only for the villa. She was intrigued by an old grapevine with a giant trunk that climbed from ground level to twine itself up white walls and around a railing of a small balcony above. Opening a gate, she found herself in a courtyard that was flanked by cypress trees, and oh, so neglected. Overgrown rose bushes rose from between broken paving stones and a broken statue of a small boy, stained and discoloured with age, was visible behind high bushes. In the centre of the courtyard a marble dolphin balanced on his tail, but no water sprouted from his mouth into a bowl discoloured with mould. Only the great stone urns cascading with pink geraniums appeared to have survived the ravages of time and neglect. Liz crushed down a feeling of dismay and disappointment.

Hadn't the Greek lawyer with the unpronounceable name—Kostas someone—warned her of the villa's state of disrepair? Or he had tried to. But it's mine, she rallied herself—well, half mine anyway, and wondered why she so often forgot about her cousin's share in the inheritance. Making her way over broken paving stones, she reached the weathered unpainted door and raised the ornamentally carved knocker.

It was very still, nothing seemed to move in the shimmering clear air. Or had she heard a movement somewhere inside the villa? She couldn't be certain. Her gaze moved to a window and a girl's face stared back at her, an anger-torn face with smouldering dark eyes. The next moment the image had vanished and presumably, Liz thought, the girl had moved to answer the door. Another lift of the knocker, however, elicited no response, and feeling piqued by the silence when she knew quite well there was someone inside, Liz kept right on knocking. Even if Katina—it must be Katina—for some reason of her own refused to welcome her here, surely someone would answer the summons. The next moment the heavy door swung open and a girl stood facing her in the opening, a remarkably lovely young Greek girl, Liz thought, even with an expression of fury darkening her aquiline features. 'Well,' hands planted aggressively on slim hips and dark head held high, 'what do *you* want?' Katina demanded fiercely. The great dark eyes in a swarthy face blazed angrily and she burst into a spate of Greek of which Liz could understand only two words, 'Katina' and 'New Zealand'. All at once the flood of words changed to English. 'You're *her*, aren't you? The one my stepfather used to tell me about.' She spat contemptuously, and her glance as she eyed Liz was pure malice. 'Go away, you are not wanted here!'

She made to close the heavy door, but Liz, sensing the movement was too quick for her and slipped inside. Crushing down the hot words that trembled on her lips, she forced her voice to an even tone. 'You don't understand. I'm your cousin and I—'

'Cousin!' Katina's tone of voice rose hysterically. 'You are not my cousin! I will never welcome you here, never!' she spat the words out.

'But—' Liz tried vainly to stem the torrent of words. Only her heightened colour betrayed her inner turmoil and her thoughts were rioting.

All at once the Greek girl broke into a storm of weeping, the tears running unrestrained down her cheeks. 'Why did it have to be you?' she sobbed. 'Why did my stepfather give you half of his property? He never told me about that.

I thought it would be mine, all mine—' She broke off to glare at Liz through a mist of tears. 'It would have been all for me but for you. Now you have ruined my life. I cannot sell my share and get the money for my dowry.' Her voice thickened, pulsing with emotion. 'It was me he should have left it to. What did you ever do for him?' she demanded fiercely.

'I used to write him letters—'

'Words, just words!' once again Katina spat expressively. 'What use are they? I was the one who helped him every day in the taverna. I looked after him when he was ill, cooked his meals, washed his clothes. And you,' her tone was infinitely contemptuous 'you didn't even know him. You were nothing to him—nothing!' The thought seemed to rouse her to a fresh surge of anger. 'Why couldn't he have left it all to me?' she cried again. 'You didn't need it! But me, I could have sold it for my dowry. My aunt and uncle, they thought I would have the dowry from my stepfather. It would have made everything right for me. I could have had many suitors asking me in marriage. Now you have spoiled it all! It's all your fault!' Her expression was so menacing that involuntarily Liz stepped backward. 'What do you know about a Greek girl and her dowry?' she flung at Liz. 'In your country you do not need a dowry, my stepfather told me. It's easy for you—' she stopped short and Liz saw with surprise that the dark anger in the swarthy face had given way to an expression of eager hope. 'You have come today about selling your share also? Together we will have the money for the sale and then—'

'No!' Now it was Liz's turn to feel indignation. 'Never! I won't do that! You'll have to find some other way of getting your dowry money.'

'Easy for you to say that,' Katina muttered resentfully. 'What do you care?' she cried bitterly. 'You come here for a holiday, swim in the sea and lie on the beach all day, bring your friends here too maybe. *Why* won't you sell?' she cried, almost beside herself with rage and frustration.

'The lawyer in Heraklion told me he has an offer. It is a chance, he said, not to be missed. But you, you will not help me, you do not care! If it was you who needed the money—'

'Listen to me! You've got it all wrong!' The hot colour flooded Liz's cheeks, but somehow she managed to speak calmly. 'I haven't any money. I just don't want to sell my share of the place, that's all.' All at once she realised how much her decision affected the Greek girl, and she added, 'But I'm sorry about your dowry.'

'Sorry! Sorry!' Katina's red lips curved in a sneer. 'If you were sorry you would sell today, this minute. Soon, let me tell you, it will be too late. But you, you do not care! Not about me, not about my stepfather either. He was nothing to you, nothing!'

Stung to anger, Liz cried, 'That's not true—' The next minute, however, she realised that nothing she could say would make the slightest difference to the Greek girl's opinion of her. Clearly Katina was beside herself with frustration and resentment—and guess who she held responsible for the twist of fate that had deprived her of her dowry at a moment when she most needed it! The thoughts churned through her mind. If only she had sufficient funds to buy out Katina's share in the estate— but that was out of the question. Clearly she wanted to get rid of Liz, and just as determinedly, Liz knew she would never give up her dream of just being here. Flinging up her small rounded chin, she looked directly into the blazing black eyes. 'Whether you like it or not,' she announced calmly, 'I'm staying right here! And if you imagine this is just a holiday trip,' she ran on, 'you're way off beam. I haven't any money, as you seem to think, only enough to pay my return fare back to New Zealand.'

'Why don't you go, then?' screamed Katina. 'You have nothing to stay for. No husband, no job to go to! Soon you will have to give up your share and sell, and then it will be my turn to say yes or no! Then you will see—'

'No!' Liz's resolute tones cut across the angry words.

'I'll find something to do to keep myself!'

'*You!*' cried Katina contemptuously. 'What could *you* do?'

'I—' Liz sought wildly in her mind for an answer. Stung to resentment by the other girl's jeering tone, she gave utterance to the first words that entered her mind. 'I'll work in the taverna, that's what!'

The swarthy hands gesticulated wildly in the air. 'You do not know what you are saying!'

'Why not?' Liz told herself that she would make a last effort at reconciliation and that would be it! 'Maybe you could help me?' She waited for a fiery reaction.

It came. 'Help you!' screamed Katina, her voice high, out of control. 'Never will I do such a thing! *You!* How could you do the work in the taverna? I cooked and cleaned and made coffee and meals and served at the tables. My stepfather, he helped me, and later on Xenia and Nikos came—'

'Okay,' Liz refused to be daunted, 'I'll try to get them to come back and work for me.'

'They have gone away,' Katina's black eyes sparkled with anger, 'and the taverna is closed. Closed! Closed! Do you understand?'

'I can see that.' Liz's gaze strayed to the deserted café with its empty seats and faded blue canvas awnings flapping in the sea breeze. 'But you made a living, you and my uncle,' she persisted. 'Lots of Greek folk must have come to the taverna—'

The moment the words left her lips she realised she had played right into her opponent's hands.

'Yes! Yes!' Katina cried triumphantly. 'With our Greek food we made a living! Our people like their own food. You—' her tone was infinitely contemptuous, 'what would you know about our food?'

'Nothing, really,' Liz admitted cheerfully, 'but I could learn.' Refusing to be daunted by the other girl's contemptuous stare, she ran on, 'I've often heard about the wonderful dishes of Greece, like rolls of minced lamb and

rice and herbs all wrapped in young vine leaves . . .
sounds delicious. And at the hotel last night—'

'Hotel meals!' Katina cut in scornfully. 'It is Greek food
altered and mixed up to please the foreigners—like you!
You had better try the food of our country before you talk
about cooking and serving it at the taverna!' She still
looked sulky and resentful, but she spoke in a quieter tone
and Liz had a wild hope that maybe the Greek girl's rage
had spent itself. Hadn't she heard that Greek folk were
volatile and changeable in mood?

'Shall I cook you a Greek dish, one that comes from our
village high in the mountains, and that way you will know
if you wish to cook such food for the taverna. You will try
it?'

Liz hesitated, taken aback by the unexpected offer. Her
thoughts churning in confusion, she wondered if this were
Katina's way of holding out the traditional olive branch.
Maybe the Greek girl was just a little sorry for her
outburst. She decided to give her the benefit of the doubt.
She wasn't at all hungry, but coffee would be appreciated.
Aloud she agreed, 'All right, then,' and catching the
sudden triumphant gleam in the black eyes, she added
hastily, 'So long as it's something plain, I never could take
black olives.' She tried for something not too highly
spiced. 'How about an omelette?'

'You like omelette? I will make one with my special
filling.'

'Oh yes, I always like omelettes.'

Katina muttered some words under her breath and Liz
found herself hoping that they hadn't been what she
imagined they had, 'You won't like this one!' The thought
sparked her to say, 'So long as they aren't too spicy.'

She might just as well have been talking to the marble
boy in the courtyard, because Katina took not the slightest notice of the remark. 'Go out to the courtyard,' she was
saying, 'there is a table there and I will bring the meal out
to you.'

Her tone was so friendly that Liz sent her a quick

glance, but the other girl's face was turned away and Liz could not glimpse her expression. 'Thank you,' she said. 'I'll just wash my hands.' As she went along the hall she could hear the rattle of pots and pans in the kitchen.

The bathroom she found to be a big cool room with taps, basin and bath and thin towels hanging from a rail. She washed her hands in the basin, then turned to the mirror as she ran a comb through her hair. How pale her face was, she thought in surprise—and she had imagined she had handled the unexpected attack of the Greek girl with complete composure! Oh well, she mused hopefully, maybe everything would turn out all right after all. If only, she reflected on a sigh, her cousin weren't such a let-down. Or had she misjudged her?

She moved through the living room with its icons on white walls and the pottery-crowded mantel and made her way out to the sun-drenched courtyard. As she stepped over the broken paving stones and dropped down on the sun-warmed marble bench at the side of a small iron table she was struck once again by the air of neglect that pervaded the area. Yet once, long ago, this had been a gracious Cretan dwelling, the entrance gates guarded by tall cypress trees and the sunny courtyard studded with marble statues. The years had taken their toll, but all the same, she cheered herself, there was still the sunshine filtering down through a screen of grapevines overhead, the little marble bench that had survived the ravages of the years, and everywhere the strangely luminous white light. Could it be because she had newly arrived from a New Zealand winter with its soft rains and cloud-enshrouded hills that the sky seemed such a tremulous, incredible blue?

All at once she spied an old stone vessel lying half hidden in weeds and, filling it from a nearby tap, she splashed water around the dust-dry roots of the struggling overgrown rose bush that somehow, despite heat and neglect, had contrived to produce clusters of fragrant white blooms. Then, stepping carefully to avoid crushing the blood-red poppies growing wild amongst the tall grass underfoot, she pulled away spent roses.

'It is ready for you.' She turned to see Katina, who was approaching her, carrying a wicker tray. Soon she had banged it down on the table and Liz saw there was a folded-over golden omelette, light and fluffy, on a plate, and a tiny cup of dark coffee served with the traditional glass of water. Katina, she thought, must have prepared the food in a remarkably short time. As she seated herself at the table Liz realised that the omelette lay in a pool of olive oil, but what matter, she could always ignore the oil, which to her palate was anything but appetising.

'Coffee? Lovely!' She took a sip of the liquid, sickly sweet and half full of sediment. Discomfitingly aware of the close scrutiny of the Greek girl, she put down the cup.

'You don't like our Greek coffee?'

Liz shrugged slim shoulders. 'Not very much. It's so strong and thick. I guess I'm just not used to it.'

Katina said nothing, but remained standing. If only, Liz thought, the other girl wouldn't watch her in that disconcerting way. Katina's narrowed gaze was a little unnerving, but maybe the Greek girl had taken trouble to prepare the dish as a peace-offering, as it were, and was anxious to have her efforts appreciated. Liz decided to ignore Katina's scrutiny and put a forkful of the omelette to her mouth. The next moment she was choking and gasping, her mouth burning and her eyes smarting— never had she tasted food so revolting! There was a strong flavour of herbs, garlic and fennel, together with spices she couldn't identify. Wildly she snatched up the glass and took great gulps of water, gasping as the cooling liquid slid down her throat, that seemed to be afire.

Still breathing with difficulty, she sprang to her feet and faced Katina's triumphant glance. 'How could you!' She put her hand to her mouth as nausea threatened, 'You made that revolting mess just to try to scare me away. It's horrible, and so are you! And if you think you can get rid of me by scaring me away with your nauseating cooking, you're way off beam. It won't work!' A flush had mounted to her delicate cheekbones and with a shock of surprise she realised her arms were trembling. As she met the malicious gleam in the black eyes she cried tersely, 'And don't think you can get me to change my mind about working in the taverna either!'

Katina let out a peal of derisive laughter. 'Stay, then! Work in the taverna, make the food my people want to eat! See if you can! I don't need to stay here. I have a friend who manages the big hotel over the hill. I have often worked there before when my stepfather didn't need me and I have a room there too. I can work there until you come to me and beg me to sell my share. My friend he has begged me to go back and work at his hotel. He knows I will take charge of the kitchen, direct the girls who do the housework, even welcome the tourists at the reception desk when the other girl is away. He is glad for me to do these things and he pays me well. So,' she screamed in sudden fury, 'stay here by yourself! See if I care! You won't help me!' she shouted accusingly 'so why should I help you!' All at once she burst into a spate of Greek of which Liz understood not one word, and throwing out a hand in a swift angry gesture, she sent the tray and its contents spinning to the ground, shattering the china to fragments and sending black olives and strong-smelling sauce spilling over the paving stones below. Then with a toss of her dark head, she flung around and hurried away.

Liz stared after her in horrified silence, one hand pressed to her burning throat. She must have been out of her skull, she scolded herself, ever to have trusted Katina. Well, she vowed, let the Greek girl try all the sneaky tricks she knew, it would make no difference. She was determined to stay here and enjoy her inheritance, no matter what! All at once her own land seemed far away and she felt very much alone in a foreign environment where she didn't even know the language, and the one person to whom she could appeal for help, the man at the hotel, was probably already on his way to another part of the island after a brief stop-over here. Anyway, she reminded herself bleakly, he despised her. He had made that plain enough last night. As for herself, she couldn't decide whether he was friend or enemy, but she couldn't help wishing she could meet him again, if only to settle the question in her own mind. It was only that charisma of his that made her think about him so often, she reasoned with herself, that and his heart-knocking appearance.

Still feeling slightly dazed by the Greek girl's unexpected attack, Liz wandered back into the house. As she entered the main room she almost collided with Katina, who came hurrying out of a bedroom, a soft embroidered bag bulging in all directions held in one hand and in the other a hairbrush and espadrilles. Clearly she was taking with her all the possessions she could carry.

'Now see how you will get on by yourself!' she hissed, and hurrying past Liz, she slammed the heavy door behind her with such force that the pottery vessels arranged along the mantel rattled alarmingly. The next moment Liz ran to the door and flung it open, watching as Katina's crimson skirt glimmered through a screen of pink oleander blossom, to vanish a few minutes later amongst the olive trees at the top of the rise.

A little later, as she took herself on a tour of the villa, she told herself that there seemed one big advantage in Greek homes. For the whitewashed walls, tiled floors and absence of clutter presented little difficulties in the way of housework. She glanced around the small room with icons on the whitewashed walls and a woven homespun cover on the bed. Evidently this had been Katina's room, she reflected, for there was a smudge of lipstick on the mirror and a drift of perfume lingered on the air. A tiny blue stone lay on the bureau. Hadn't she heard Greek girls used them as charms? The kitchen she found to be a sunny room with a colourful tiled floor and an old black stove above which hung bunches of dried herbs, rosemary, thyme and sage. She shuddered at the unpleasant aroma clinging to a blackened frying pan to which some sauce still adhered.

But thank heaven, she thought, her uncle had evidently recently been connected with electricity, for a shining new range and kettle appeared scarcely to have been used. A swift glance along the open shelves revealed a stock of essential foodstuffs, flour, sugar, tinned milk—instant coffee. Goody, goody! And wouldn't you know—massive containers of olive oil! Liz wrinkled her small nose at the sight of jars of black olives—a luxury food where she came from in the South Pacific but one she had never developed a taste for, and after today's episode, she knew she never would!

She opened a door from the passage and found herself in a sparsely furnished bedroom. Could this have been her uncle's room? It was difficult to know, as someone had removed all traces of personal belongings. There was just a narrow bed, a shabby chest of drawers, a faded woven rug on the tiled floor. There was nothing to tell her if he had used the room. A pity, for she would have liked to have had something of his, just as a keepsake. Absently she opened a drawer of the wooden chest, but it was empty. The next moment she realised she had been mistaken, for tucked away at the back of the drawer and evidently overlooked by whoever it was who had tidied away his possessions she found a bundle of letters. Her eyes misted over as she recognised the childish writing. To think he had kept the letters she had written him all through the years! Suddenly a photograph fell from the open bundle, herself as a smiling thirteen-year-old. Heavens, she mused, how plump she had been in those days! For a long time she pored over the handwritten pages, then at last she replaced them in the drawer and went to get her travel pack. As she threw it on the bed she reflected that for the first time she was beginning to feel a little at home here. The small balcony-room upstairs with its vine-encrusted terrace was inviting, but she knew that this was the room she would use for herself.

Happily she began draping dresses and tops on hangers and hanging them on a rail. Her brief blue bikini she

tossed on the bed, promising herself that as soon as she
had a look through the taverna below she would christen
the garment in the sapphire sea she could see from the
window. She lost no time in hurrying over the long grass
and down to the sand, already warm to the touch of her
bare feet. Soon she was crossing the concrete strip and
unlocking the weathered door of the timber building, to
find herself in a long room with a counter built along one
wall. Woven baskets held stocks of glasses and pottery
mugs and a drawer below the counter took care of the cash
takings. Liz pushed open a long shutter, to find herself
looking out on a sun-drenched scene where waves
creamed in soft curves on the stretch of sand. She turned
away and crossed the room to open a swing door leading
into a kitchen. Her glance roved over a blackened stove,
heavy pots and pans and long benches. Open shelves were
stocked with cooking materials and on the wall hung
bunches of dried onions and tomatoes. As she had heard
was the custom in Greek dwellings, everything was immaculate. All at once she spied a doorway that opened
into a small room where whitewashed walls were hung
with icons with their oil dips. There was a wooden table, a
couple of rush chairs, rough bunks covered with woven
spreads. Up till this moment she hadn't realised that the
taverna held living quarters—but then, she mused on a
sigh, there were so many aspects of her uncle's life that
were unknown to her. Had this room, she wondered, been
the home of the Greek couple who had helped Katina in
the taverna during the owner's illness? But she didn't wish
to dwell on the Greek girl. She'd think instead of a swim in
the inviting blue water below.

Although it was early in the day the heat was increas-
ing, and back in the villa she went to her room and
slipping out of her garments, pulled on a pale blue bikini,
then threw over her head a loose dress of soft Indian
cotton printed in muted tonings of crimsons and blues.
Soon she was making her way to the courtyard. Already it
was her favourite spot and once she had cleared away the

long grass ... She had stooped to pull aside the encroaching weeds from around the marble statue when a masculine voice from behind arrested her. 'Hope I'm not too early for you. I just called in to—'

Liz froze. Her heart was behaving strangely, and all at once bells were ringing all over the place. That voice! That deep, vibrant, *unforgettable* voice. She straightened and spun around to face brilliant dark blue eyes in a deeply tanned face. Realisation came to both at the same moment, and in an instinctive reaction their voices merged in a cry of delight and astonishment, 'It's you! It's really you!'

CHAPTER THREE

'So—' she found herself enmeshed in his brilliant gaze, 'we meet again. Adam's the name, Adam Farmsworth! And you're Jim Kay's niece, Elizabeth?'

Liz smiled up into the strong dark face. Somehow she was finding it easy to smile right now. 'That's right. But I usually answer to Liz. How did you know about me?'

He laughed. 'The local grapevine functions pretty well around here.'

'Oh!' All the time her mind was registering how attractive he was, in a casual, sun-bronzed sort of way—the athletic figure, the strength of the masculine face with its black-lashed eyes and sensitive mouth. Oh, she had just known that he would be like this, seen in the hot white light of day. Aloud she heard herself say stupidly, 'I didn't think I'd ever see you again!'

'That goes for me too!' His deep tones were still tinged with pleasure. She caught the veiled amusement in his glance. 'Moonlight becomes you. Did anyone ever tell you?'

She could feel the tell-tale colour creeping up her cheeks and hastily she changed the subject. 'I wanted to see you—just to thank you.' Suddenly it seemed very important that she should put matters straight between them. 'You do understand about last night?' Her grey-blue eyes, clear as a child's, swept up to meet his gaze, 'It's true what I told you . . . it was just an accident. You do believe me?'

He grinned and she caught the flash of teeth, extraordinarily white against the dark tan of his skin. 'Why do you think I called the night porter?'

'You took your time about it.' She couldn't resist the jibe.

'Can you blame me?' His dark blue eyes held a lively

expression. 'The Cretan moonlight is very revealing.' At the glint of amusement in his gaze, the colour in her cheeks deepened, but now she knew it was only amusement. The note of contempt in his tones that had so distressed her last night had gone, replaced by warm appreciation. 'I looked for you at the breakfast table this morning.' Heavens, she thought, aghast, why am I letting my tongue run away with me like this? Swiftly she added, 'Just to thank you.'

'I never eat breakfast,' he sent her a grin, 'but if anyone offers me coffee round about this time of the day—'

She smiled back at him. 'I'll see what I can do!' All at once the scene around her seemed to shimmer in the crystalline air. Or could that be her imagination? 'I've only just moved in here today, all the way from a New Zealand winter.'

Again she glimpsed the glimmer of laughter in his eyes. 'So that's why your shoulders are so pale.'

She refused, however, to allow herself to be drawn into that particular trap by his mocking voice. 'Not for long. I haven't had a swim in the bay yet, but that's my first priority—after coffee, of course!' She took in his sun-bronzed limbs, the cotton shirt open to the waist revealing his tanned torso and the dark line of his swimming trunks. 'Do you often come over here to swim?'

'All the time.' His tone was careless. 'I happen to live around here, just over the hill. It's no distance over the goat track.'

Liz turned away. 'Come into the house and I'll fix coffee.' Together they strolled into the coolness of the villa and Adam Farmsworth followed her down the whitewashed hall and into the kitchen. A fresh breeze, spiced with an aroma strange to her, drifted in at the open window. 'Nice,' Liz sniffed appreciatively. 'What is it? Do you know?'

'An aromatic herb called dittany that grows only on the island—I'll give you a hand.' He was taking coffee mugs from hooks on the wall and putting them on the table. Then he found instant coffee on a shelf. 'Goodness,' said

Liz in amazement,' 'you've been here before!' A sudden thought occurred to her and she looked at him excitedly. 'If you live around here you would have known my uncle.'

'That's right.' He was watching her fill the electric kettle from the tap. 'Nice old boy. I used to drop in to see him now and again. Only one thing wrong with him,' was she imagining a sharper tone in his voice, the lazy laughter in it quenched? 'he was pigheaded as they come. Once he'd made up his mind to anything,' he threw up well-shaped bronzed hands, 'you couldn't shift him. That was it. Finish!' His tone changed to a teasing inflection. 'Don't tell me that you take after him?'

She rushed to his defence. 'I never found him to be that way at all! Anyway,' she said with spirit, 'lots of folk call that strength of character.'

Adam shrugged broad shoulders. 'Whatever it was, there was no arguing him out of anything once he'd made up his mind—Hey!' he looked at her in surprise, 'I didn't know you two had ever met! He used to talk about you a lot, but he never put me in the picture about that.'

Liz shook her head. 'Only in letters. We corresponded for years and years. You'd be surprised how much I know of his life in Crete.'

She caught a sudden flicker of interest in his dark blue eyes. 'Like what?'

'Oh, local customs. Friends he'd made on the island, all those things.'

'I get it.' He appeared to have lost interest in the matter. 'So long as you don't take after him,' he grinned, 'in "strength of character", as you call it.'

She threw him a teasing look. Somehow it was easy to talk to him on this sundrenched day in exciting, unfamiliar surroundings. 'Would it matter so much?'

All at once in a swift change of mood, he was withdrawn, serious.

'It could to me.'

Her eyes widened and she stared up at him in amazement. 'What do you mean?'

'Forget it!' He took the mug of coffee she was handing to him, then went to perch on the scrubbed table, swinging a long tanned leg. 'Katina told me all about you months ago. She didn't ever expect you to make the trip out here.' He shot her a grin. 'Staying long?'

Such a matter-of-fact enquiry, yet to Liz the words seemed to hang in the air with an odd significance. It *must* be her imagination. 'As long as I can! I'm fascinated by this island,' she said confidingly. 'I have been for years. It was just so terrible Uncle Jim dying before I could get here. I'd been saving up for the trip to Greece for years, and then when I did finally get here, my uncle wasn't here any longer and Katina, my cousin—' she pulled a face 'I call her my cousin, but she's only a "step" really—'

'Didn't put out the welcome mat for you, I gather?' Adam said, grinning.

Liz shrugged slim shoulders. 'Anything but! She made it fairly plain that she doesn't want to have me around, refuses to have anything to do with me. It's awkward,' she stirred her coffee thoughtfully, 'when we both have shares in the place. Oh well,' she said with more confidence than she felt, deep down, 'maybe she'll change her mind in time.'

'Actually she called in to see me this morning. She's often worked for me—'

At last the penny dropped. 'Now I know where you live! At the hotel!'

He nodded. 'I run the show and staff difficulties can be a problem. Luckily Katina lives fairly close and I can always call on her in an emergency. She's worked for me on and off since last summer when I was looking for someone to superintend the kitchen staff and keep the household side of things ticking along. I've found her to be first class, and she happens to speak English, so when she turned up today wanting employment at the hotel it suited me fine. Now that the summer season's starting I'm in luck having someone on the staff like Katina, whom I can depend on.'

Liz's mouth fell open and she said incredulously, 'Depend—on Katina!'

He laughed at her expression of amazement. 'Sure, why not? Oh, I grant you she can fly into a fury half a dozen times in a day, Greeks are like that. They can carry on like nobody's business one minute and be the best of buddies the next! It's a national characteristic, you'll get used to it!'

'Maybe,' Liz said doubtfully. She was finding difficulty in imagining the Greek girl being really friendly with her—ever. She brought her mind back to his deep tones.

'So here you are all on your own on a Greek island on the most fabulous holiday that anyone could wish for—' He broke off and shot her an enquiring glance. 'Or is it just a holiday?'

Liz got a strange impression that her answer was in some way important to him, but she told herself that was ridiculous. 'I'm going to play it by ear,' she told him, 'coast along for a while and see how I get along.' No use confiding to him at this early stage the exciting solution to her financial problems that had just this moment flashed into her mind. It was an idea, she thought jubilantly, with infinite possibilities, but one she would need to think over carefully before making her plans public. Her glance went to the window with its vista of hazy blue hills. 'It's so beautiful here—'

'With the best swimming beach for miles.' Adam grinned. 'Why don't we try it out? It's a waste of time being in the bay without taking a dip.'

She laughed. 'I'm all ready—well, almost. Just give me time to put on some sun-lotion. Won't be a minute!' She found her Greek bag and tossed into it a bottle of lotion, tinted sunglasses and a towel, worn and freshly laundered, that she found in a drawer.

Adam was waiting for her in the bright sunlight of the courtyard, holding out towards her a bunch of white grapes he had plucked from the vine clinging to the sagging supports. 'Try some! They're recommended! Your uncle was no end proud of his *rosaki* grapes.' He was watching her as she sampled a sun-warmed delicious grape. 'He always said—' He broke off, his gaze resting on the low scooped neckline of her sun-frock. 'You are sun-tanned, after all!'

Acutely conscious of his gaze, Liz rushed into speech. 'This is just a winter tan, left over from summer. In Auckland, where I come from, the city's bang between two huge harbours and there are so many lovely swimming beaches you wouldn't believe! It's not like here, though, where the tides don't seem to vary much. Pretty soon I guess I'll have my Cretan variety of suntan. A swim every day, that's what I've promised myself. Maybe two.'

'Great! I'll join you!' The words were carelessly said, yet they sent her spirits soaring.

Still plucking at the grapes in her hand, she went with him over the strip of grass and down on the sand, warm to her bare feet.

'Looks dreary, doesn't it?' She glanced towards the taverna they were passing. 'Empty tables, folded sun-umbrellas, closed doors! I had ideas that Katina and I might run it between us,' she confided, 'but she didn't go for that one little bit! Anyway,' all at once she was conscious of a surge of pure happiness, 'I'm not worrying about that right now.' Her glance went to the sandy shore, washed by a translucent sea.

When they neared the shoreline Adam paused to take off his light cotton shirt, tossing it down on the sand, and she took in the supple strength of his chest and wide shoulders, sun-darkened to an even tan. The next moment she pulled her sun-frock over her head and threw it down. 'Beat you in!'

She sped away, bare feet flying over the sand and her hair streaming behind her shoulders. He caught up with her at the water's edge and together they plunged into the foaming sea. 'It's gorgeous!' Liz cried, delighting in the warmth and buoyancy of seawater that caressed her skin like the touch of silk. Soon they waited their chance to drop down on an incoming breaker to be carried into the shallows, then wade through a frothing sea back into deeper water. At last they swam out into the deep. A moderately good swimmer herself, Liz had to admit that Adam's powerful crawl as he sliced through the water was a delight to see. Just for fun she waited until they paused to tread water, then swam a short distance away, calling back over her shoulder, 'Race you to the rocks at the end of the point!'

'Right! You're on!'

She was hopelessly outpaced, of course, she knew that from the start. Indeed, the distance was farther than she had imagined and before long her strength was flagging, though she would never admit it. All at once he was at her side, but instead of moving ahead, he grasped her arm. 'Take it easy. Had enough? Those rocks are a hell of a lot farther away than you'd think! Come on, I'll practise my life-saving act and we'll head for the shore!'

Liz hadn't any breath left to answer him, but she turned to float on her back. The next moment she felt his strong arms around her, then he was propelling them through the water.

'Wow!' She dropped her feet down to firm sand. 'I don't know what happened to me. I really thought I could make it.' She pushed back the wet curtain of hair from her face. 'Just as well you were there!'

He laughed. 'Your own fault for throwing challenges around!'

'I know, I know.'

They dropped down on the towels they spread on the sand and lay back, letting the dazzling sunshine stream down on their faces. It was a world of their own where the only sound was the gentle murmuring of the waves and the cry of seagulls wheeling overhead. Time ceased to matter and she was conscious only of a delicious lassitude and an odd sense of belonging. No doubt she felt that way, she thought dreamily, because of having no folk of her own and becoming so attached to this uncle in Crete. The

singleminded determination to get here had given her the
necessary strength of mind to forgo new clothes, entertain-
ments, expensive make-up, anything that might cut into
her hard-won savings. All the time, deep down, she had
been aware of a hazard that could well put an end to her
dream. She knew that whatever happened she mustn't
allow herself to get too deeply involved in a romantic
relationship. Fortunately, she congratulated herself, the
decision to end a promising love affair that she had made
on two occasions in the past hadn't really worried her
unduly. How could it, when her own private dream
beckoned ahead?

She stole a sideways glance at Adam, whose eyes were
closed and she could take her fill of looking at him,
something she was finding she enjoyed a lot. Could she
have dealt so resolutely and lightheartedly with a blos-
soming romance had the man who loved her devotedly
been Adam Farmsworth? Now where, she asked herself
the next moment, could that absurd thought have sprung
from?

Lulled to a companionable silence by the dazzling
sunshine that was drying the salt on their bodies, she was
conscious all over again of a feeling of dreamy content. She
raised herself a little, leaning on her elbow and once again
letting her gaze rest on Adam. He was lying on his back,
his arms crossed behind his neck. There was a special
magic about him, she mused—the thickly-growing dark
hair, the erect lean body, the eyes that seemed so full of
light. He was a man, the thought came unbidden, that a
girl would find it all too easy to lose her heart to, if she
weren't on her guard!

All at once she realised his eyes were open, just a slit but
sufficient to reveal the glint of amusement in his sideways
gaze. Thank heaven, she thought, her face was already
flushed with the touch of the sun and disguised the hot tide
of colour running up her cheeks. Forgetting all about her
resolution not to divulge her plans, she rushed into
speech. 'Guess what? I'm going into business!'

'What!' All at once he was alert, interested, his tone questioning. 'I got the idea you were over here on an extended holiday. You mean you're leaving the villa, going to stay at Chania or Heraklion?'

His sharp tone sent a tingle of excitement flicking along her nerves. Could it matter to him, so much, so soon? Would he really miss her if she left the villa? The thought was intoxicating and she raised herself to lean on an elbow, looking down at the sand she was sifting through her fingers so he wouldn't catch the expression of happiness in her face. 'No, no, you'd never catch me leaving here.'

The urgency in his gaze died away. 'That's all right, then.' At his sudden relaxation she felt again that flicker of joy. 'You don't seem much interested in my project,' she complained.

'You haven't let me in on it yet, but if you're planning on selling crocheted lampshades or handmade cushions—'

'Don't worry,' said Liz, 'All I'm doing is to carry on the family tradition. I'm going to open up the taverna.'

'You're having me on!' His incredulous expression was anything but flattering to her ambitions.

'What's wrong with my having a go at running it?' Her eyes were dreamy. 'There was this nice Canadian woman, she was staying at your hotel when I was there, and she gave me the idea.'

'You can't be serious!' He was eyeing her with amusement. 'You don't mean you're taking that on, Greek cooking and all?'

Her eyes fell before his mocking glance. It must be because of his dark blue gaze, so penetrating and full of light, that she couldn't sustain his look. 'No Greek cooking!'

'What, then?'

'Would you believe? Good old English tea and American coffee and chilled fruit drinks. It will be something different for the tourists—'

The lurking amusement in his eyes deepened. 'It won't,

you know! Tourists can soon find that sort of thing if they know where to look for it!'

'Aha,' she cried triumphantly, 'but not right here, with homemade rolls toasted and served with the filling of their choice!' As always when she was feeling enthusiastic about anything, her huge grey-blue eyes glowed with excitement. 'The Canadian lady I met had been to Greece lots of times, and she really did seem to know what she was talking about! From what she said I gathered that Greek food is fine for people who appreciate it (she gave an involuntary shudder at the remembrance of the supposedly native dish prepared especially for her by Katina), but lots of tourists especially the older variety, miss the foods they're accustomed to having at home. Oh, I know it sounds awfully stupid and plain and downright boring to you,' she hastened to say, 'but in a way I can understand how they feel.'

Warned by the discouraging expression in his eyes, she ran on before he could argue the matter. 'Oh, I know that the equipment I'll need for a start-off will cost me plenty. I'll have to have a freezer, a cabinet with lots and lots of glass-topped compartments and a toasting machine. I'm so lucky having electricity already installed at the taverna and the villa—' A sudden thought flashed through her mind. 'I guess I've got you and your hotel to thank for that! So,' she pretended not to see the disapproval in his eyes, 'if you feel like a cup of good old English tea—sorry I can't promise to provide anything stronger—you'll know where to find it! You look a bit off-putting,' she chided him smilingly. 'What's wrong with it, for heaven's sake?'

'If you want it straight,' his face had sobered, 'you could find yourself up against a few financial problems. Away down here miles from the towns it isn't easy to arrange deliveries. There'd be hefty cartage as well as installing costs.'

'Oh, that's all right!' She refused to be discouraged by his unhelpful attitude. 'I'm so lucky! Uncle Jim gave me my return fare to Greece. Being here suits me just fine, and

I can easily use the money for the return fare and pay myself back later.'

He pinned her with his unrelenting blue gaze. 'No going back?' There was a glint of amusement in his eyes. 'What are you planning on doing? Going to marry a Greek?'

'No!' she protested hotly, and realised the next moment it was the very reaction he had hoped to provoke from her.

'Not a Greek?' he enquired blandly. 'You'd prefer—'

Lis dropped her eyes before his gaze. 'Not any man! At least—'

'You don't seem very sure about it.'

'You know what I mean! What I mean to do,' she rushed on breathlessly, 'is to pay myself back from the profits I'll make this summer!'

Adam squinted into the clear blue bowl of the sky. 'And if you don't make a profit, what then?'

'Stop!' She threw her hands up and cupped her ears. 'You're just trying to ruin my plans!'

He took not the slightest notice of her protest. 'For a kick-off you'd better realise right here and now that you could be billed for a lot more drachmas than you're counting on for the stuff you need. Then you'll need help in the kitchen—'

'Who says so?' She flashed him an impish grin. 'I've made up my mind to go it alone!'

He threw her a sceptical look. 'Your uncle used to employ a Greek couple who worked in the kitchen at the taverna. Katina used to give him a hand too—'

'And now she works for you!'

'That's right.' His tone was noncommittal. 'One of the few Greeks on my payroll who can speak English fluently. That means I can rely on her to fill in at the reception desk when the regular girl is away.'

Liz was scarcely listening. She was sick and tired of being forced to listen to his praises of Katina. All at once she found herself wondering if the Greek girl had told Adam of her arrival at the villa. Katina had flounced off in such a rage that she had probably given him a colourful account of the confrontation between herself and Liz in the courtyard. Or had she? In view of the rapid changes of mood that seemed to be characteristic of Greeks, Liz had a faint hope that the other girl may have calmed down by the time she arrived at the hotel. One thing was for sure—Adam wasn't giving anything away in that direction. Still, the question continued to nag at her. 'Did Katina tell you that I was here?' The words seemed to come without her volition.

'She mentioned it.' He appeared scarcely interested in the matter. Maybe, she thought, he was accustomed to Katina's emotional outbursts and took little notice of her excitability. She wrenched her mind back to his deep tones. 'That's why I came over to see you today, just to say hi!'

'Hi!' She smiled across at him. 'So you don't think much of my project?'

'Not much. You could end up by running up debts you couldn't meet, get in too deep.'

'I won't—'

'It's on the cards,' he pursued inexorably. 'What would you do then?'

She refused to be deterred by his negative attitude. 'I don't know!' Then, on an inspiration. 'Get a loan from that lawyer in Heraklion, I suppose. Kostas someone—I never can pronounce his name. He said to ask him if I needed any help with anything at all. I'm sure he would arrange something for me through the bank.'

You could tell by his expression, Liz thought, that Adam didn't think much of the idea. He said briefly, 'You'd be so lucky!'

'He promised to help me. And he seemed awfully kind . . .' The words faltered into an uneasy silence. She had a disquieting suspicion that a girl who was going it alone in a strange land would be more than a fool to put herself under an obligation to the Greek lawyer. There was something about the intimacy of his hot, dark eyes . . . She thrust the uneasy thoughts aside. It wasn't as if she would

ever need to ask him for monetary help to tide her over.
She'd manage somehow, of course she would!

She brought her mind back to Adam's admonishing
tones. 'So long as you don't let yourself in for more than
you bargain for!'

It was precisely the thought that had been going
through her own mind, but she had no intention of giving
him the satisfaction of letting him know. 'I thought maybe
you'd help me,' she wrinkled her nose at him, 'tell me the
name and address of the shop where I can send in my
order for the equipment I need.'

'Right, I'll give it to you later. You can get it all in
Heraklion.' He sent her a sharp glance. 'Except the
kitchen help you'll be needing. You'd have to go to the
village for that.'

'You keep going on about it,' she complained, 'and I
keep telling you I don't need anyone else. Anyway, I'll
worry about that one when I come to it!' The sundrenched
day, the dreamy sense of relaxation laced with the heady
excitement of the man at her side with his lean tanned
body and sardonic expression, all conspired to go to her
head a little and she heard herself saying happily, confi-
dently, 'It'll all work out, you'll see! Anyway,' she threw
back the long damp hair from around her face, 'you
shouldn't be doing your best to discourage me from
opening up the taverna. Just think of your middle-aged
clientele,' she threw him a teasing smile, 'who'll come
hiking over the hill just for some good old plain filled
restaurant rolls, as a change from your horrible Greek
dishes at the Hermes dining room—'

Adam rose to his feet and stood looking down at her. 'I
take that as a challenge! Take it back or I'll have to make
you—'

'You'll have to catch me first!' Quick as a flash Liz had
leaped to her feet and dodged between his sinewy arm.
'Race you to the water!'

She was barely a step ahead of him as she splashed into
the foaming tide. The next minute he caught up with her

and catching her up in purposeful arms he carried her out to deeper water, then—'No!' She was kicking and struggling in his grasp, but he took no notice but dumped her unceremoniously in the water. She emerged with streaming hair, breathless, dashing moisture from her eyes with the backs of her hands. 'Just wait until I catch up with you!' She took after him, then stopped to tread water, breaking into laughter. It was that sort of heat-hazy day, and soon they were making for the shore together.

Much later when at last they splashed through the shallows after another dip in the sea, Liz paused to wring out the long dark rope of her hair. 'Heaven only knows what the time is! I—' Her voice died away as her gaze rested on Adam, his thick black hair in curly disorder, drops of seawater glistening on his muscular tanned chest. With an effort she wrenched her mind back to his voice. What was he saying? she wondered wildly. Something about having to meet someone, a builder who was coming to see him about making alterations to the structure of the hotel. 'He'll be waiting for me now, I guess.' Reluctantly they made their way over the sand, warm to the touch of their bare feet, past the empty taverna and up to the villa. Somehow she hated to see him go, and on an impulse she said, 'Oh, you were going to let me have the name and address of the electrical firm in town, maybe they'll supply the cabinet with the containers as well.'

For a moment he was silent. Then, 'Over to you. You'd better get a quote from them before you do anything drastic.' Moving into the living room of the dwelling, he went to a cabinet and took out pen and paper. He knows where everything's kept here, Liz thought once again, and wondered just how well Adam had known her uncle.

He handed her a slip of paper. 'You can drop your letter in at the hotel for posting any time,' she caught the hard note of disapproval in his voice, 'that is if you insist on going through with your scheme!'

She pulled a face at him. 'You're trying to knock me—spoil everything!'

'Would I do that to you, Liz?'

'Well, you do your best to pour cold water on my ideas all the time.'

His tone softened. 'Someone's got to look after you. You're in Greece now and the Greeks believe in protecting their womenfolk, especially the unmarried girls—'

She wrinkled her nose at him. 'But you're not a Greek!'

'As good as.' The warmth in his brilliant eyes seemed to deepen. 'You know the old saying, "When in Rome . . ." Tell you what, I'll pick you up on Sunday and we'll take a look at Aghios Nikolaos, it's a picturesque little village down the coast—that is if you've nothing else on?'

'No, no! I'd love that!' Did she sound as excited as she felt about the invitation? To try and tone down the eager happiness in her voice she added, 'I've got to make the most of my free time here. Once I get going with the taverna—'

'Oh yes, your taverna—'

Swiftly she picked up the satirical note in his dry tone. 'Why do you say it like that? Don't you think I can make a go of it?'

'Frankly, no.'

'Why not?' she demanded.

Adam shrugged broad shoulders. 'Just a matter of good old drachmas. If it was a matter of carrying on like your uncle did you might pull it off, but even then you'd need a lot of help.'

'My uncle managed well enough,' she said stiffly. She added reluctantly, 'Of course he had Katina to help him—well, some of the time.'

He grinned. 'And the Greeks who used the rooms at the back of the taverna . . . nice old couple. They knew the place inside out and he'd have managed fine with them, even without Katina's help.'

'I see. When did they go away from here?'

'They stayed on until just before you came, the taverna was closed for the winter anyway, and went to live in the village. You'll have to meet them some time, you'd like

Xenia and Nikos. Honest as they come, and loyal as hell to your uncle.'

All at once her eyes were alight with enthusiasm. 'Maybe they'd come back and work for me?'

'Sure they would, they'd come like a shot.'

'Of course, I couldn't afford it right away, but maybe later on when I get the money—Oh, I know what you're thinking—more drachmas, and I've barely enough to get started—but don't worry, I'll get the money to put myself in business.' And she spoiled the brave statement by adding a trifle uncertainly, 'Somehow . . . you'll see.'

'Don't worry about it!' His grin was infectious. 'You're in a country that's new to you, all set to explore one of the loveliest villages in the Greek islands—'

With a man who I'd rather be with than anyone else . . . anywhere! The thought came unbidden.

CHAPTER FOUR

LIZ was feeling so excited about the trip to Aghios Nikolaos with Adam that she awoke very early in the morning. 'It's really me,' she exulted, 'I'm here in Crete at last, about to go with Adam to Aghios Nikolaos!' The name rang a bell in her mind then she recalled viewing with breathless interest a TV series entitled *Who Pays the Ferryman*, filmed in that particular village in Crete.

A glance through the window showed her a luminous blue sky giving promise of a hot day to come, and she chose a dress of cool white cotton printed with green palm trees and the word 'Paradise'. The dress she had brought with her from New Zealand seemed to fit the occasion, for what could be more exciting than to be taken by Adam to the locale of *The Lotus Eaters*? She wandered into the kitchen, where she mixed a mug of instant coffee, made a tomato sandwich for herself and nibbled some of the goat's milk cheese she liked.

Today she decided she wouldn't use much make-up, just sun-lotion and waterproof eye make-up. The excitement glowing in her eyes was there for all to see, but what matter? Soon she was slipping into her capacious Greek bag her blue bikini, camera, towel, comb and sunglasses. Then, fitting her feet into woven string sandals, she made her way out to the courtyard to wait for Adam.

It was very still, the only sound the waves washing up on the beach below. A small lizard clung motionless to the whitewashed wall. Idly Liz plucked the spent blossoms from a rose bush growing wild, the thorny branches spreading high overhead, then she decided to take a snapshot of the courtyard to send home. But *this* was her home now, the thought flickered through her mind. At least, that was the way she already felt about it. It was amazing.

She was snapping the picture when a car pulled up outside and the first she knew of Adam's arrival was the sight of his tall figure approaching her.

She greeted him with her wide smile. 'Hi! This picture is for the girls in the office, back home.'

'Now I'll take one of you!'

'Oh, would you?' She glanced up, eyes alight. 'They'd never believe how lovely it is here unless I send them some evidence to prove it, broken fountain and all!' She offered him her tiny Instamatic, but he waved it away.

'I've got my own, that way I can be sure of getting one for myself!'

Delight vibrated along her nerves, but she made her voice casual. 'If you really want one?'

Liz found the answer to her question in the warmth that had leaped into his eyes. 'All right, then.' She stood motionless, trying not to blink against the bright sunlight. She had no need to force a smile. Trouble was, she thought, she couldn't seem to stop smiling today!

The next moment she caught the click of the shutter. 'Got it!' said Adam with satisfaction. 'All ready to go?'

'I've been ready for ages!' Why must she say things like that, she scolded herself inwardly, betraying all too clearly the heady excitement she was feeling?

A little later, seated beside Adam in his long red car, she was conscious once again of a surge of pure happiness. 'It's the day,' she assured herself, 'and the air, this crystal-clear air.'

'And being with Adam,' her heart supplied.

She wound down the car window and the light breeze blew softly over her face, stirring the dark hair at her temples and bringing with it an elusive aroma, something she couldn't put a name to.

He seemed to tune in on her thoughts. 'Bet you don't know what that tang is in the air?'

'I haven't a clue. It's something new to me.' She laughed with a sheer joy of living. 'It's all new to me here.'

'A lot of different herbs grow over the hillsides.'

She laughed again. 'I'm learning all the time!'

They took a road winding up a slope that was sparsely covered with the silvery green of olive trees and bright with blood-red poppies, white daisies and small blue wildflowers growing along the roadside. Far ahead Liz could see the hazy blue of distant hills. The next moment she realised they were swiftly overtaking another traveller on the road, a swarthy Greek man seated on the wooden slatted saddle of a donkey while a woman wearing long dark skirts, her face shaded by a black coif, walked alongside. 'Well,' breathed Liz indignantly, 'just look at that! I suppose the woman hurrying alongside the donkey is the Greek's wife?'

Adam threw her a grin. 'No Women's Lib in the villages around here!'

'I think it's awful, his poor wife having to trot alongside the donkey! I thought you told me—' She turned towards him, her words dying into silence as she took in his tanned profile, clear-cut as if cast in bronze. It was amazing the pleasure she took in just . . . looking at him. With an effort she pulled her thoughts together and said hurriedly, '—that womenfolk in Greece are protected and looked after by their men?'

'True. But after marriage they're expected to work out in the fields, tending the grapevines, working in the olive groves, gathering the herbs. The hours are long and hard and the hot sun of the Greek islands doesn't do much for their complexions.'

'I can see what you mean.' Liz recalled the sun-dried, nut-brown faces of the women working in the fields. Maybe, she thought, they weren't as old as she had thought but prematurely aged by a burning Cretan sun and endless physical toil.

Adam's eyes glinted with amusement. 'Don't look so het-up about it! I hear that the women do have one day off a year and on that day they kick the men out of the tavernas and instead of the men sitting around there all day, drinking endless cups of Turkish coffee and playing with their worry beads, the women take over!'

'Good for them!'

'It's not a bad idea, the Greek way—' She surprised a teasing light in his eyes.

'Oh, you would say that!' she disclaimed. 'You're a man!'

He said dryly, 'You've noticed?'

Oh, she'd noticed all right. She couldn't seem to keep her gaze from straying endlessly towards him, taking her fill of looking at the lean dark face and eyes that didn't miss a thing! What if he should suspect the way she was feeling about him right at this minute? The possibility was so unnerving that she broke into speech, saying the first words that came into her mind. 'All those black clothes the Cretan women wear—they look as if they're in perpetual mourning!'

His eyes were fixed on the winding highway ahead.

'Blame the sun for that too!'

'And with all that,' she marvelled aloud, 'Greek girls still need to produce a dowry to find themselves a husband! They do, don't they? It seems so far back in the past, that sort of thing!' She was thinking that she wouldn't put it past Katina to tell her any old lie that would serve to get her what she wanted.

'Do they ever? It's the custom of the country,' he explained. 'Seems to work well enough in this part of the world. You've got to remember that a Greek man doesn't get very high wages, either before or after marriage.' He grinned across at her. 'But you still don't go along with it?'

'No, I don't!' she said with spirit.

He only laughed and sped on. Soon they were taking a smooth highway cutting between hills covered in low-growing olive trees, to drop down to a plain planted with olives and almonds. Presently they passed a tour bus crowded with sightseers, then merged into the line of cars moving ahead of them. Then all at once they rounded a curve, and looking down on the scene outspread below, Liz drew a sharp breath of delight.

'It's so beautiful,' she breathed, leaning forward to take in the vista of a seaside town that appeared to be built around a deep circular lake. Pleasure craft met their reflections in the still depths and blue and white sunbrellas shaded tables and seats of tavernas set at the water's edge. The narrow winding streets were lined with small stores. Liz caught sight of proprietors standing in doorways while embroidered muslin dresses swung on hangers around them.

Adam guided the car down to the lake's edge, manoeuvring the vehicle amongst cars and tour buses to find a parking space in the crowded area. Soon he and Liz were strolling down a narrow winding street where each store displayed attractive ornaments and locally made souvenirs. The scene sparkled in the clear white light and presently, a hand on her elbow, Adam guided her down a street where store displays breathed wealth and opulence. The treasures seemed endless—porcelain and pottery, small urns made in the style of the originals. It was, however, the golden glitter of a small jewellery store that held Liz's fascinated gaze. She had never owned anything but a few pieces of costume jewellery, had never even been tempted, but there was something about this bright Greek gold . . . She looked at the glittering jewelled amulets and earrings and hair ornaments, all fashioned with exquisite craftsmanship and made with a simplicity of design that could have belonged to the stylised form of today.

'Come along inside and take a closer look.' A hand laid on her warm tanned arm, he piloted her into a room that breathed wealth and luxury and the patronage of an international clientele.

Liz paused before a glass display case, attracted by gleaming necklaces fashioned in triple curves of Greek gold. Somehow, she mused, the gold seemed to gleam with a special lustre. Just like the air here, the sunshine—all at once she was very much aware of Adam's nearness—her own golden day! Aloud she commented, 'Isn't that the style worn by Greek maidens thousands of years ago?'

'Sure is. Lots of these ornaments are copies of treasures unearthed by archaeologists—tell me, which is it to be?' He was teasing her, of course, he must be, Liz thought as he ran on, 'A silver slave bangle, emerald earrings, a pearl-studded comb for your hair?'

Smilingly, she shook her head. 'All far too expensive.'

Leaning an elbow on the counter, he studied her with lazy detachment. 'But if you had a choice?' he persisted.

'Well,' she smiled up into his tanned face, 'if I had all the money in the world I wouldn't go for any of those, where on earth would I wear them? But this . . .' Her voice died away as her gaze went to a thin gold chain from which hung a tiny golden bee, its jewelled wing and sting tips attached by the finest of gold wires. 'I've seen pictures of the original,' she told him, looking up at him excitedly. As she met his deep brilliant gaze she wrenched her glance aside and heard herself floundering in a tumble of words. 'The pendant of the bees, it was called. And it's at the Museum at Heraklion.'

'That's right. The famous Minoan Golden Bee pendant. The archaeological boys found it not so long ago, amongst the ruins of a king's palace. Luckily it was surprisingly preserved. I'll take you to see it, if you're interested.'

'Oh, I am, I am! I'm interested in anything, everything in Crete.'—*So long as I can see it with you.* The thought came unbidden. She brought her mind back to his deep vibrant tones.

'We haven't started our sightseeing tours yet. I know the island so well.'

He was speaking, she thought, on a wave of excitement, as though the future held many more meetings, as if he had in mind taking her to the many places of interest that abounded in this most fascinating of Greek islands. There was a warmth, a special something in his eyes when he looked at her that made her think he felt the same way about her as she did about him.

'Right,' he was saying, 'that's it, then! I'll get it for you.'

'Me?' She was taken by surprise. 'Goodness, no! It must cost the earth!'

'Not really. It's not the original, you know!'

'I couldn't let you,' she protested. She had a dreadful suspicion that he might have imagined she was hinting for the pendant.

'Why not?' He sent her the heart-knocking grin she found so difficult to resist. 'Give me one good reason.'

'I told you, it's too pricey!'

'Well, that's out for a start!'

'I mean—' something in his bright steady gaze was sending happiness pulsing through her, making it awfully difficult to concentrate. She said the first words that came into her mind. 'It's not as if it were just a little souvenir.'

'What else?'

She could feel the hot colour running up the apricot tan of her cheeks. Heavens, she thought with dismay, what if he imagines—? The next moment, however, she realised that he was pressing home the advantage she had handed him. 'You must have a souvenir. Something to take back with you from Crete.'

She twinkled up at him. 'What makes you think I'm ever going back?' All at once she realised that a man and girl standing nearby were taking an interest in the conversation and hurriedly she said, 'All right, then, if you insist.' At that moment an assistant stepped towards them, as if on cue, or had he too been an interested listener of her and Adam's words? she wondered. The money changed hands, then Adam slipped the small jeweller's box into the pocket of his jacket.

As they went out into the hot sunshine of the pavement Liz said, 'You shouldn't have done this. I didn't want—'

'Yes, you did! I could tell by your face! It's nothing, just a small souvenir.'

She eyed him suspiciously, uncertain whether or not to believe him.

'Well,' she said at last, 'if you're quite sure—' In spite of herself she couldn't keep the note of excitement from her voice. 'Let me see—'

'Sorry, but you'll have to wait!' Liz felt she could drown in the brilliant light that was flooding his eyes. 'Until you can thank me properly.'

'I can thank you now!'

'In the street? I know a much better place. You'll just have to be patient.'

She wrinkled her nose at him. 'It's unfair! I haven't even seen the original and you have! Lucky you!'

'Lucky!' Adam took her arm and they strolled on down the sunshiny street. 'I've been to that museum so many times I just about know every exhibit that's there off by heart.'

Swinging her bag, she paused to look at him in surprise. 'I had no idea you were a student of Greek mythology.'

'I'm not, but my father was. He earned his living teaching languages at university and he was absorbed in Greek mythology. For years my parents spent their holidays in the Greek Islands, studying temples and buried treasures and amphitheatres. As a kid I didn't go for it much, but later on I used to manage to get a holiday job in the holidays in Greece, so I guess something of my dad's interest in the country must have rubbed off on me after all.' All at once his face sobered. 'He died suddenly, a year after my mother, leaving me enough capital to start some sort of business. I'd spent a few years managing tourist hotels around the holiday spots in England, and I decided to take a chance and put all the money I had into building a big luxury place somewhere by the sea in Greece. Crete had always been my dad's favourite Greek island, and somehow I felt that investing the money this way would be something that would have appealed to him. Not as much as helping to finance a new museum of Greek artifacts, of course, but I couldn't handle that. The way I figured it, I wanted a spot away from the usual tourist circuit, a place where guests could relax and do their own thing, sit around the bar, try out Greek food in the villages, hire a car if they wanted to and explore the coast. I got together with an architect friend in London and we drew up the plans together. We both agreed on the main points—lots of space and air, a marble staircase to the first floor, lounge and bedroom windows to look right over the sea. The Greek builders took their time putting up the place, but it's finished at last.'

'And things are working out all right for you?'

'Financially, you mean?' He shrugged broad shoulders. 'This is my first season and the summer travel trade hasn't got into full swing yet, but if a special plan of mine turns up trumps—'

Liz looked at him enquiringly. 'Special plan?'

He brushed the matter aside. 'It's a long-term thing, so I'm just keeping my fingers crossed!'

They sauntered on down a twisting narrow street, pausing to look in at windows of tiny stores with their displays of woven floor mats in brilliant shades of reds and yellows, Turkish slippers with turned-up toes, miniature bouzoukis, richly decorated coffee cups, vessels that were replicas of pottery unearthed from the ruins of buried cities. There were florist shops, fragrant with growing greenery, art shops exhibiting paintings so expensive that Liz gasped at the price tags. She recognised a glamorous-looking woman strolling by as a famous American movie star.

'One could meet people here you only read about at home,' she told Adam.

He said with a grin, 'According to Greek mythology, Athene used to bathe in the little lake here.'

'I don't wonder. This must be one of the loveliest villages in the whole world,' Liz breathed.

He smiled down at her. 'Depends on who you happen to be with!'

Her heart shouted assent, and as they moved over the sun-dried plaza she felt her spirits rise on a tide of elation. For a moment the scene before her, the blue enclosed lake, the passing crowd, shimmered with a feeling of heightened perception. 'Make it last,' she prayed, 'my wonderful, wonderful day!'

'Where would you like a meal?' Adam's deep purposeful tones wrenched her back to mundane matters. 'At a taverna down by the lake or bread and cheese on the beach?'

'I'll settle for the beach every time!' The prospect, she thought, was entrancing.

'Me too.'

They wandered up a winding, narrow street, to pause, attracted by an appetising aroma of newly-baked bread that drifted out through an open doorway. Inside the shop were loaves of all shapes and sizes, still hot from the oven. Farther along the street, Adam purchased a bottle of the local wine, and soon Liz's bag was bulging with bunches of white grapes, feta cheese and great yellow Cretan oranges.

Suddenly, at the top of the rise, they came in sight of white cottages tumbling down to the sea. Below, bikini-clad girls and men in swimming shorts were lying sunbathing on the golden sands washed by the Aegean Sea.

A little later they changed into swimming gear and left their garments together with Liz's bag beneath a shady tree on the grassy bank. Soon they were running together over smooth sand to plunge into water so warm and buoyant that meeting the surge of the waves was no shock at all. Not half such a shock to Liz as when Adam swam up behind her to duck her in the water. She came to the surface with streaming hair, dashing seawater from her eyes, and immediately gave chase, but of course it was hopeless trying to catch up with him.

Later they spread towels on the warm sand and let the hot sunlight play on their bodies, lulling them into a state of dreamy content. After a while Adam appeared to have fallen asleep and she turned towards him, acutely aware of his lithe tanned body lying so close. All at once impelled by a longing to touch him, she stretched out her hand, to find her fingers imprisoned in his warm grip. For a

moment the sundrenched scene shimmered around her
and a wild happiness pulsed through her. How could his
touch electrify her like this? Swiftly he flung himself
around and kissed her full on the lips. In his eyes she
glimpsed a glint. 'That's for starters!'

Suddenly nervous of the effect his caress had had on
her, she got to her feet. 'What's the matter, Liz?' He was
regarding her lazily through half-closed eyes.

'Nothing, nothing!' Murmuring something about
lunch, she moved away, making her way between the
sun-umbrellas that dotted the sand. The thoughts whirled
through her mind. How could he affect her in this way, a
stranger about whom she knew nothing? It's the day, she
told herself, and as he caught up with her she managed to
get her runaway emotions under sufficient control to
school her voice to a light note. 'I thought you wanted
to sunbathe a bit longer?'

'Not without you beside me, Liz.'

She sent him a swift sideways glance from under her
eyelashes, surprised to find that he was perfectly matter-
of-fact. He really meant what he'd said! Once again the
warm happiness surged through her.

It was a meal to remember, Liz decided a short time
later, as she munched happily on freshly baked bread. If
this were a sample of Greek food she was all for it. Not
like—Determinedly she switched her mind away from
Katina and the nauseating dish she had prepared special-
ly for her. She refused to allow thoughts of Katina to dim
the radiance of her day with Adam. The Cretan oranges,
she thought, were like no others she had ever tasted and
the wine, with its delicate flavour of almonds, was delicious.

Afterwards they sunbathed once again on the warm
sand and time ceased to matter. It was a day to plunge
into the azure sea, then relax on the beach. To run down to
the water once more, to laugh and splash each other and
float with faces upturned to the sky on the buoyant
sun-sparkled sea. The hours drifted by and it was a long

time later when the lavender light of a Crete twilight crept
over the darkening sea and they watched the night fishermen climb aboard their boats and guide their caïques
into the sunset.

As they made their way back to the main square of the
village the soft purple twilight deepened into darkness and
lights sprang up in the clusters of white cottages running
down to the sea. The narrow twisting lanes were alive with
music and as they came into the square they found the
streets lined with onlookers as they watched Cretan dancers in their colourful costumes, the women wearing white
muslin blouses and dark red skirts with necklaces of gold
coins swinging around their necks.

Liz was enchanted as she watched the Cretans sweep
into their wildly energetic dances to the lively beat of their
native lyre. She held her breath as male dancers linked
hands with their girl partners, swinging them off their feet
and whirling them through the air, embroidered skirts
flying around them in a wild crescendo.

Much later, Adam escorted Liz through the crowd.
'Would you care to try out a little café I know along the
coast, or would you prefer that I took you to a restaurant
for a meal?'

'Oh no, the café will be fun!' *Everything is fun when I'm
with you, Adam!* she thought happily.

The haunting music of the lyre drifted out to them as
they moved away from the main square. Dimly lighted
tavernas threw a glow on the dark street and soon they
had reached the parking area. Adam saw Liz into the car
and they turned into the main road. Presently he drew the
vehicle to a stop at the side of a dimly-lit café. As he
escorted Liz to the open doorway she hesitated, laughter
glimmering in her eyes. 'Are you sure women are permit-
ted in here?' She caught echoes of bursts of masculine
laughter and loud talk and peering inside she dimly
discerned, in the faint blue glow, a crowd of swarthy male
faces. 'It's not one of those all-men tavernas I've heard
about?'

'With all those international tourists cluttering up the place?' Adam urged her forward, a hand on her arm. 'Come in and meet my friend Nikolaos.' As they made their way through the crowded room, he said, 'He owns the show, and he'd be no end offended if he couldn't show us himself what he's offering on the menu tonight.'

An aromatic, appetising smell of cooking greeted them as they went into a kitchen where Greek men were busy cooking food at a blackened stove.

'Adam!' At their approach an older man swung around, his swarthy face beaming. He broke into an excited spate of Greek, nodding every now and again towards Liz, who did the best she could with an answering smile. She had no need to know the Greek language to understand that Nikolaos, with much gesticulating and loud talk, was inviting them to make their choice from the foods steaming in smoke-blackened pots. All at once, as the group moved towards the stove, Nikolaos's face darkened. His dark eyes flashed angrily and he waved both hands wildly in the air. 'What's he saying?' Liz whispered to Adam. 'Don't say we've offended him in some way?'

'Good lord, no! He's apologising for the lack of fresh fish today.'

'But he sounds so angry—'

'He is. He says the fishermen of the village sold their entire catch today in the market in Athens. But he can recommend the pilaf, soups, dolmades—'

'Dolmades!' Liz clapped her hands. 'Isn't that a gorgeous dish wrapped in vine leaves that I'm always reading about? I'd love to try it!'

'Right! You won't be sorry you ordered it, Nikolaos will see to that!' He gave the order to the Greek owner of the café for egg and lemon soup followed by dolmades.

Nikolaos escorted them to a table and Liz, casting a swift glance around her, took in the raftered ceiling and smoke-darkened walls that were lined with huge wooden wine barrels. Now that her eyes were becoming accustomed to the smoke-filled room she realised that, as Adam had told her, there were other women seated around her, well-dressed Greek women accompanied by their escorts and parties of overseas tourists who were no doubt staying in the colourful village.

Around them groups of Greeks talked argued and roared with laughter. With their dark aquiline faces and black moustaches, wearing black beaded kerchiefs on their foreheads and jackboots on their feet, they looked, Liz thought, like brigands. All at once she became conscious of a noisy group of Greek men at the next table who were laughing and talking loudly as they gesticulated excitedly in her direction. 'Those men at the next table,' she whispered to Adam, 'I know they're talking about you and me.' His eyes glinted with amusement and she ran on indignantly, 'And it's no use your trying to tell me they're not, because I distinctly heard them mention your name and then they all turned around to look at me. You heard what they've been saying,' she accused him indignantly, 'I can tell by your face! Come on, tell me, what did they say—about us?'

He sent her an enigmatic look. 'You really want me to tell you?'

She smiled back at him. 'Can't wait!'

'Prettiest girl in the room,' they said. His eyes held a glint of amusement. 'They wanted to ask the waiter to give you wine with their compliments, but they weren't quite sure about that, thought they might have a fight on their hands, because anyone could see that you weren't just a dinner companion but something much more. That you were my *gheñeke*—'

'*Gheñeke?*'

'My woman.'

'Oh!' Liz was taken aback in spite of herself and tried for lightness. 'I'd like to know,' she said in the most nonchalant tone she could summon up, 'just what gave them that idea.'

'They said,' he announced calmly, 'it was the way we look at each other.'

Now she didn't dare look into his eyes. She managed a brief laugh that even to her own ears didn't sound genuine. 'Is that all?'

Adam said quietly, 'Isn't that enough?'

Liz didn't know whether she was relieved or sorry when at that moment a young Greek boy brought soup, steaming hot, in bowls made from local pottery.

'Like it?' Adam was eyeing her attentively.

'It's delicious.' He was beckoning to a waiter, saying something in the boy's native tongue, and she guessed he was ordering wine. 'Cretan Minos,' he told her. 'You'll like it, I promise.' When it came to the table she sipped the sweet wine with enjoyment.

The stuffed vine leaves too, with their filling of minced lamb and delicate flavour of herbs, she found delicious. 'I'll have to get the recipe,' she told Adam with her quick smile. 'If I'm going to stay on here there's lots of things I'll have to learn about.'

'You're still counting on staying, then?' She sensed an odd note in his voice.

'As long as I can! I was telling you, all I have to do to make a living is get myself going with toasted rolls in the taverna my uncle left me and I'm away.'

All at once his voice hardened. 'And if you can't make a go of it—'

In the moment of silence the thoughts raced through her mind. There was a sort of listening look on his dark goodlooking face, as if it mattered to him a lot whether she stayed in Crete or not. The wild sweet happiness tingled along her nerves, for that meant that he was interested in her, that he cared about her. Maybe even he had plans that included both her and himself. The thought was so intoxicating that she had difficulty in bringing her mind back to his deep resonant tones. 'What if you can't get your project off the ground?'

She wrinkled her nose at him. 'Oh, don't be so dampening! If it's finance you're thinking of—'

'It is, actually.'

'I told you,' she said airily, 'that my lawyer will see to that. He told me he'd give me some help if I got into any difficulties.'

Still Adam appeared unconvinced, regarding her thoughtfully. 'But if he doesn't?'

She laughed with sheer exhilaration. 'I'll tell you one thing, I'm not leaving my villa!'

'Yours?' Once again she caught the strange, enigmatic note in his voice.

'Well, half mine,' she admitted reluctantly. Why must she keep forgetting about Katina's share of the property? she asked herself. Some trick of the mind, because she wanted to forget? But she refused to allow herself to be discouraged on this exciting night out with Adam. 'I'll find something to keep me going,' she said lightly. At the wry twist of his lips, his disbelieving glance, she added, 'I don't think even the Oracle at Delphi could answer that one offhand! Don't look like that, all disapproving,' she begged him. 'I'll think of something! Maybe,' she teased, 'if all else fails I'll join in the evening parade down the village street that I've heard about, where the girls dress up in their prettiest frocks and the boys may look but not touch. The *volta*, isn't that what they call it? The bride market?'

Her laughing gaze rose to his and as their glances met and held tiny flames seemed to glow in his eyes. Hurriedly she dropped her gaze, unable to sustain his brilliant look.

'You won't need to do that, Liz.'

She would need to watch her words, the thought came through the confusion of her senses. There was something about this man that affected her as no other man had ever done. He made life so different that a Crete village became a place of enchantment, a dimly-lit café was shot with magic.

They lingered over the Greek coffee, rich and strong, that had been served with a glass of water, watching as a Greek man at a nearby table got to his feet. The next moment his rich notes rang out to the accompaniment of the plaintive notes of a lyre.

'What's the song about?' Liz whispered.

'Poetry the Cretans have set to music,' Adam explained, 'all about the ups and downs of love.'

'Love?'

'That's right.' His glance rested on her downcast face and he asked softly, 'Know anything about it, Liz?'

She flashed him a laughing glance. 'Do you?' The thought ran through her mind that he was a man apparently in his early thirties, very presentable, rich, attractive. He must have had affairs, even perhaps a wife.

Adam seemed to pick up her thoughts. He was twirling his wine glass, his eyes veiled. 'I was married once. Eleni was Greek. We were both young and we thought we had it made. Just goes to show how mistaken you can be.' His tone was thoughtful and he seemed to have forgotten her, Liz thought. 'I took Eleni back to England with me and we'd only been married a year when she was killed in a car smash—one of those freak accidents. She was driving with a friend to the local shops,' his eyes darkened, 'when a drunken driver met them head-on on a bend and both the women were killed instantly. That happened a long time ago, and I've never found anyone to take Eleni's place—' his sombre glance lifted to Liz's face, 'yet.' All at once he was back to his impersonal manner. 'Well, that's me— How about you?'

She sneaked a look at him from under her lashes and took a sip of coffee. 'Nothing!'

'Nothing? Looking like you do?' His warm appreciative glance swept over her wide blue-grey eyes, alight with excitement, the sweetly curved mouth and short nose. 'I don't believe it.'

'It's true,' she answered smilingly. 'I guess I'm just not the falling-madly-in-love type,' she added, and made the mistake of looking up, directly into those brilliant eyes that seemed to possess the disconcerting knack of being able to read her mind. She looked away, fearful he might read in her glance the feelings he aroused in her. 'I have to admit,' she ran on, saying the first words that entered her mind in order to cover her confusion, 'there could be a reason.'

'And that is—?' His attentive gaze was fixed on her face.

Thoughtfully Liz stirred what was left of the coffee in her tiny cup. 'Believe it or not, it was Crete!'

He sent her a sceptical glance. 'Don't give me that! You'd never even set foot on the island.'

'But that's just it—don't you see? I was so wrapped up on the place. It was Uncle's letters from here that started it and kept going my obsession, I suppose you could call it, alive for me all those years. I read every book about the island that I could get my hands on, found out all I could and saved every cent I could for the trip.' She raised clear eyes to his attentive gaze. 'I guess I must be a pretty determined type after all,' her lips twitched at the corners, 'because I wouldn't let anything or anyone—especially any man—' she spread her hands expressively, 'stop me. Know what I mean? I just wouldn't let myself get too involved with anyone, that way I knew would be the end of my dream.'

'Funny girl!'

'I know it sounds silly, but that's me! It was just as well that my uncle arranged the trip for me,' she ran on with a rueful smile. 'I'd been out of work for ages and my savings had just melted away. I was just starting on another "get myself to Greece fund, no matter what" when the letter arrived from the solicitor in Heraklion. I suppose,' she finished on a breath, 'you think I'm crazy to get so obsessed by a place I'd never seen.'

To her surprise Adam grinned. 'Why should I think that? We happen to be two of a kind. I haven't any ideas of leaving this island. It's got something, and whatever it is, it draws you back.'

But you can afford to live anywhere in the world you wish. Liz said the words silently.

She sipped her wine. 'You know something? Sometimes I can't believe I'm really here.'

He grinned. 'You've got that excited look in your eyes again!'

'Can't help it! It's all so—so far away from anything I've ever known. Everything's new and exciting—' Especially you. The words came to her mind of their own volition and she lowered her lashes, fearful of what her expression might betray. But apparently she need not have concerned herself on that score.

'I can take you to lots of other places well worth a trip,' Adam was saying. 'A sail to one of the smaller islands around here, a look at the Palace at Knossos.' His smile drew her into a warm intimacy. 'Stick around for a while and I'll show you one of the mountain villages.'

'Oh, I'll be here! Anyway, you'd never believe it, but I have to look up a family in a mountain village on this side of the island. My neighbour at home comes from there, and you should see all the goodies she's given me to take to her family. Lots of photographs of her Kiwi husband and their two children too. Angeliké will have written to her people letting them know I'm coming to see them, so I'll have to make it soon. I guess it's a big event in their lives, getting first-hand news of their daughter and son too, from someone who knows them both so well. It's a village called Kaminaki and it's way up in the mountains. Does the bus go there from our part of the world?'

Amusement glinted in Adam's eyes. 'There is a bus, but it's pretty erratic—quite an experience, that bus trip to the mountains, actually. Why bother when I'll be picking you up and we'll take in a drive to the village? It's quite a sightseeing place up there.'

'Oh, I didn't mean that!' she protested in some confusion.

'I did! A pleasure, Liz, especially when you open wide those big eyes of yours and get such a kick out of everything. Better watch it,' he grinned, and threw an arm around her shoulders, 'the way you're going you'll never get back to New Zealand!'

She pulled a face at him. 'Who said I wanted to!'

'You've made your point—want to dance?'

'Dance?' She was bemused by the wine and the music, the noise, the dark aquiline faces all around her. Now she realised that Greeks and tourist visitors were forming a circle, hands laid on one another's shoulders. The beat of the lyre was slow and measured.

'Come on.' Taking her hand in his, Adam drew her to her feet but Liz pulled back. 'I can't do the Greek dances, I don't know the steps—'

'There's nothing to it,' he assured it. 'It's the *stae tria*, the Greek dance that everyone knows and can pick up. Just remember there's a lot of one, two, three, kick, kick—there's the leader who puts everyone in the picture!' With arm thrown around her slim waist, he guided her to the laughing group who were still forming a circle. Diffidently Liz took her place between Adam and a burly Greek with an impressive drooping black moustache and a ferocious expression. Adam's arm tightened around her with an encouraging squeeze. 'Put your hand on my shoulder and follow my steps, then it's easy.' At that moment the beat of lyre music quickened in the smoke-filled room and Liz found herself giggling helplessly as she attempted to follow Adam's lead. She quickly picked up the pattern of the simple dance steps and along with the rest of the incomplete circle, kept in time with the rhythm, although she couldn't even attempt to emulate the young Cretan leader whose wild leaps and skips were apparently accomplishments of his own.

'You're doing fine,' Adam encouraged.

'Think so?' Never would she admit that being with him was doing things to her that made the simple steps of the Greek dance of little importance.

All at once the music of the stringed instruments picked up, changing to a quicker and quicker tempo until the dance came to an end and Liz, still breathless, returned with Adam to their table.

As she sipped her wine she was aware of his warm glance. 'Enjoying it?'

'Oh *yes!*' She leaned an elbow on the table, looking across at him, her eyes dreamy. 'I guess you could say that I'm in love with this island.' *I'm in love with you!* It was almost as if she had said the words aloud, and swiftly she lowered her lashes to hide the expression in her eyes. Could this be love? she wondered. This wild sweetness that was coursing through her veins, the longing she felt to trace the outline of Adam's firm, sensitive mouth with her fingers? It's the wine, she told herself, the music, that's making me so I can't think straight.

As the hours slipped by the Greek dancing became more unrestrained, the music of the stringed instruments louder, and Liz suspected the songs that accompanied the lyre were bawdier. Greeks were noisily talking, laughing, arguing and a Greek woman was climbing up on a table to dance. The next moment Liz caught the sound of a plate crashing to the floor, then another.

'Time to go, by the sound of it!' Adam's voice was matter-of-fact. Together they pushed their way through the shouting throng in the smoke-filled room, eventually moving with tourists towards the door and out into the clear night air. In the dim light Liz glanced at her wristwatch. Four o'clock! And the night wasn't yet ended, because ahead—the thought was intoxicating—was the long drive back to the villa, a perfect end to an unforgettable evening.

When they reached the village, lights gleamed on craft anchored in the tranquil waterfront and only a few cars were standing in the car park. Adam saw her seated in the vehicle, then folded his long length into the driver's seat, then they were leaving the village and turning into the darkening road that curved over the hills. They were alone on the dark highway, and when he threw an arm around her shoulders, she nestled close to his chest. They didn't talk much on the journey. Liz was in a blissful state of deep content, and the moon riding high in a star-ridden sky was only a part of the enchantment.

She enjoyed being with Adam, she mused happily. She enjoyed looking at him too—she stole a glance at the strong masculine profile, shadowy in the dim light of the dashboard. When at last they came in sight of the soaring white building against the backdrop of a dark sea, Adam guided the car towards the main entrance and leaping to the ground, went around the vehicle to open the passenger door for Liz. 'I'll see you back to the villa.' He clasped her hand in his warm grasp and they made their way along the dusty white path winding amongst the olive trees.

CHAPTER FIVE

ALL too soon, Liz thought, they had reached the secluded courtyard and as they paused in the shadows Adam drew her close—so close that she could feel the warmth of his sinewy chest through the thin fabric of his shirt. He bent his head to drop light butterfly kisses that brushed her forehead, the tip of her nose, then his seeking lips found her mouth. Fire was singing along her veins and she was scarcely aware of her own ardent response to his caress.

At last she stirred in his arms. 'I've got to go—'

'Maybe you'd better,' his voice was deep with emotion. 'You won't forget our date next week?'

As if she could!

'Pick you up on Tuesday,' his tone softened, roughened, 'that is, if I can wait that long! How about a trip to Knossos? Buried palaces that have been unearthed after four thousand years are a part of your education on a trip to Greece.'

Over the rioting of her senses Liz was scarcely aware of what she was saying. 'I'm not one for visiting old ruins, but when you put it that way—'

'So long as I've got you with me,' gently he raised her fingers to his lips, 'what matter where we go?'

Liz could scarcely believe her ears. Zeus, coming down from the heights of Mount Olympus, preferring the company of an ordinary mortal like herself to the wealthy international visitors with whom his work brought him in constant contact!

'I'll see you soon,' she murmured, and slipped from his grasp.

His low tone halted her. 'Haven't you forgotten something?'

She hadn't really, but she made a pretence of having done so. 'Oh, you mean——?'

'I mean your Minoan honey bee. Come back here, young Liz,' he said softly, 'and try it on for size!'

He looked very tall and impressive, the thought ran through her mind as she turned back towards him. The next minute he was putting a hand to the pocket of his jacket, then he slipped the fine chain of the pendant over her dark hair. Once again his nearness was doing things to her composure and she heard her own voice saying breathlessly, 'You'll never see to do it up,' but already his deft fingers had secured the fastening and in the pale gleam of fading stars she caught the golden gleam of gauzy wings.

'It's lovely, lovely,' she whispered, fingering the tiny stylized bee. 'I didn't need it, though,' she added very low, 'to remember today.'

'Liz——' All at once Adam's tone was husky with emotion. She felt his breath on her face as he gathered her close, then her arms linked themselves around his neck. The next moment his mouth was on hers, sending her senses spinning wildly. He took his time about his kiss on her soft lips, and Liz felt as though she were drowning in waves of deep sweet happiness. She clung to him, her lips responding in a torrent of feeling. Then abruptly the moment was shattered, for in another part of her mind she had realised that a light had flashed on in a room in the villa and a girl's face was visible at the uncurtained window.

'What's wrong?' asked Adam.

'It's Katina!' she gasped. 'I've just seen her at a window. What on earth is she doing here?'

'Probably wondering what's happened to you.'

'Me? She doesn't care one little bit about me!'

'Maybe,' his voice was careless, 'she came back here for something she left here and decided to stay the night.' Liz's mind went to the small blue stone on the bureau 'It's her home too,' he reminded her gently. 'Guess she's got a right to come back here now and again if she gets bored with hotel living. Don't worry about her. She'll be back at work at the hotel in an hour or so. She won't hang around the place, not a chance.'

'I guess not.' Somehow the spell was broken, and a chill sense of foreboding touched her. Trust Katina to spoil the happiest day she had ever known! 'I'll see you soon,' she whispered, and gently Adam released her.

'Night, Liz.' He turned and strode away into the shadows.

The sense of deep happiness enveloped Liz like a cloud as she neared the door of the villa. The warmth and passion of Adam's kiss was still with her, and she had forgotten Katina—until the Greek girl came out of the bedroom and stood in the lighted room. She had evidently been asleep, for she wore a light wrap over her slim body. The dark eyes that regarded Liz were sulky and resentful.

All at once Liz became aware of tousled hair and flushed cheeks. She just knew she had the soft dreamy look of a girl who had just been kissed by a man with whom she was falling in love, why not admit it? The thought made her say the first words that entered her mind. 'What are *you* doing here?'

'What are you?' Katina's lips curved contemptuously. 'It is my house too!'

'You could have told me you were coming—'

'Why should I?' demanded Katina. 'You couldn't stop me!'

It was true, Liz admitted to herself. Why, oh, why had the other girl chosen to come here tonight, ruining everything, making a nuisance of herself?

'I come and go as I please! I'll go out with Adam too, when he asks me. And when he does,' venom dripped in her tone, 'it will be because he wants me to go out with him,' infinite scorn tinged the mocking words, 'not like you!'

Liz was conscious of a niggling sense of unease, but she thrust the feeling aside. Katina was just being vindictive, of course, making up some wild story for her own ends.

Aloud she said coldly, 'What do you mean, not like you?'

'Can't you see for yourself?' screamed Katina. 'You must be as blind as the bats in the mountain caves!'

But Liz was becoming impatient with the Greek girl and her histrionics. 'See what? I've no idea what you're getting at!'

'He didn't tell you, then,' a vindictive note of triumph coloured the words, 'what he told me? We used to talk about it a lot before you came to Crete.'

'Talk over—me?' Liz was so taken aback she forgot to be angry. 'How could Adam have done that? He didn't know anything about me.'

Katina tossed her head so that the black hair swirled around her shoulders. 'Stupid, stupid, New Zealand girl! He knew all about you!'

All at once Liz let out her breath on a sigh of relief. She must have been out of her mind to fear anything the Greek girl could tell her, or to take any notice of the veiled insinuations. 'Of course Adam knew my uncle. He told me he used to talk to him. Uncle would have told him about having a niece in New Zealand.'

'Do you think Adam cared about that?' The words came on a scornful breath. 'All he cares about is getting the villa and the taverna for himself. He made an offer through his lawyer to buy it from you, he knew I would be agreeable. Long before you came here, he wrote to the lawyer in Heraklion offering lots and lots of money.'

Liz felt stunned by the other girl's words, her mind feverishly trying to escape the import of the conversation. 'Are you telling me,' the words came slowly, dragged from a pain-filled well deep inside her, 'that Adam is the hotel owner who made that offer?'

Katina's glittering angry eyes said it all. 'Who else would want to buy this place so far from any town?'

Liz clutched at a shred of hope that entered her mind. 'But it couldn't possibly be Adam. He already has a brand new luxury hotel he's built around the point. Why would he want another one so close?'

'Not another hotel, stupid! It is the bay he wants for his tourists, so that they can swim and take walks and enjoy themselves on the beach. So quiet, so peaceful, he said, away from the big cities of Crete.'

'You're crazy!' Liz's tone was low and distraught. 'I don't know why I listen to you!'

Katina's dark face was thrust so close that instinctively Liz recoiled from the other girl's nearness. 'Because you know that I speak the truth, that's why! What do you care,' she ran wildly on, 'that I don't have my dowry in money now when I need it? When men want to marry me and my aunt and uncle, they have to decide. All you care about is yourself!' The spate of words flowed around Liz without her being aware of them. Only one fact registered in her mind. There must be some mistake, she told herself doggedly. Aloud she said, 'He would have told me!'

'Told you! Told you!' jeered Katina. 'Why would he do that when all the time he knew you would say no, no, no, like you always do! The day you arrived here, I told Adam that you were crazy about keeping the property and staying on here. Do you know what he said to me?' Without waiting for an answer she swept on, swarthy hands gesticulating. '"Do not concern yourself, Katina. Be patient and soon, I promise you, all will be changed, and you will have your dowry. I haven't met this girl yet, but when I do I'll soon talk her into my way of thinking. I've got my methods and I'll be able to persuade her to change her ideas."'

Persuade her, persuade her! The words beat a dull tattoo in Liz's mind. The other girl's vindictive tones seemed to be coming from a distance, 'Soften you up? Isn't that what you call it? And you think,' came the sneering tones, 'that he likes taking you out, being nice to you! I tell you it is all a trick to get his own way. He is making you get fond of him in the ways of a man. So easy for him,' the contemptuous gaze flickered over Liz's rumpled hair and hot cheeks,' when already you think he is some sort of god! You will see, when the time is right, he will get from you what he wants,' the cruel words were arrows aimed straight for the heart, 'and then he will think it was worth all the trouble he had to take to make you love him!'

'Stop!' Liz covered her ears with her hands. 'You've never wanted me to come here, so you're telling me all these lies!'

'Lies, you say?' Fury exploded in the dark eyes. 'Did he tell you that he had a wife once, a Greek girl who he took to England with him to live? He likes Greek girls.' Without waiting for an answer she swept on. 'No, it is only to me he speaks of such things. She died in England and since then he is alone, he can please himself. Why should he waste his time with you,' she hissed 'when he can have any woman he wants,' she snapped her fingers in the air, 'just like that! It is only that you are so stubborn, so stupid about money matters, that he has to pretend to like you!'

The flush had died away from Liz's cheeks, leaving her very pale. A cold resolve took the place of shock and anger. 'I don't believe you!'

'Why don't you sell your share, then,' a cunning gleam had flashed into Katina's dark eyes, 'and see how much he wants you then?'

'I'll never sell, don't you understand, never, never, never!'

'You say that so that you can keep him hanging around you, pretending to like you. That is all it is with Adam, just pretending!'

A black tide of anger mushroomed up inside Liz and spilled over. 'You're making all this up!' Lifting her chin, she pushed past the Greek girl and made her way to her own room. Katina's voice, high, out of control, echoed in her ears. 'Ask him then if you don't believe me! Ask him! Ask him!'

Liz threw herself down on the bed, not bothering to undress, shock and disbelief struggling in her distraught mind. She watched the trembling of her hands as if they belonged to another girl. It wasn't true, it couldn't be true that Adam was cultivating her friendship for purposes of his own! A gleam of hope struggled through the dark confusion of her mind. She suspected Katina of being capable of inventing any wild story that might serve to frighten Liz away from the villa. Of course it wasn't the truth, she assured herself. Adam really did like her for herself, of course he did!

Close on the thought came a sickening reminder. Hadn't she brushed aside the lawyer's attempt to acquaint her with the name of the would-be buyer for the property here? She had taken it for granted that the hotel owner in question would be a Greek. If only she had listened to the lawyer and become familiar with the man's name she would know the truth for sure. *You know already.* The thought welled up from the deep recesses of her mind. For who else but Adam with his recently constructed palatial building, so close to beach and villa, would have an interest in the place? Small things, insignificant in themselves and unnoticed at the time, returned to mind to pierce her with painful clarity. Adam's deep vibrant tones as he said to her, 'If my plans work out—' 'Plans?' she echoed. She hadn't really been listening, because at the time she had been more interested in him than in his evasive answer to her query. What had he said? Something about a 'long-term' plan. Another thing, the daunting manner in which he had reacted to her confidences about her staying on in Crete, starting up the taverna again in her own way.

It isn't true, it can't be true what Katina told me about him, she thought. She would say anything just to get rid of me. But deep down where it counted she knew there could be no mistake. It was all too clear now. There was but one luxury hotel in the vicinity and only one owner who would have an interest in acquiring the beach property. So much interest, in fact, that he had offered an extremely high figure in an effort to acquire it for himself.

It all added up to a sickeningly inescapable conclusion. Liz lay very still, sick with shock and pain and a searing sense of let-down. Adam his traitor's smile, his lively challenging eyes that looked at you so straight that you believed without question every word that he said. And all the time . . . Unconsciously her fingers went to the tiny golden bee hanging from its fine chain. *The bee with a sting*, she reminded herself and, suddenly angry, she tugged the pendant roughly over her hair and tossed it into a corner of the room. So much for dreams. If only she had used her brains and hadn't been so naïve. Fool, she chided herself, you've played right into his hands! I suppose I'm lucky, she told herself with tight lips, that I've found him out in time. Otherwise I might even have fallen in love with him.

What do you mean, 'might'? jeered a small voice deep in her mind.

Nonsense! How could I love a man who's been only pretending to like me for myself?

What else do you call it? She thrust the insistent voice aside and, scarcely aware of her movements, flung off her garments and reached for her nightdress. No! Not that one! All at once her glazed expression had flickered into life, for she held in her hands the pale green wisp of nylon that she had worn on the night she had first met Adam. Hurling it angrily to the floor, she fumbled in a drawer for a white cotton nightdress and crawled between the sheets.

It was then that the tears came, great choking sobs that racked her body mercilessly. She buried her face in the pillow, fearful that Katina might catch the sound of muffled sobbing.

As she lay there, her eyelids swollen with weeping, it came to her that Adam's plans of 'softening her up' had misfired only because Katina had let out his intentions. Why had Katina done it? Could it be that the Greek girl's volatile temperament had made her temper fly out of control? That, beside herself with jealousy and resentment, Katina had taken her own method of revenge? It was unlikely that she would confide in Adam, so no doubt he would imagine that his plan of campaign was succeeding, as it had done. Up to a point, Liz assured herself hastily. It was left to her to let him know that she knew all about his underhand methods of doing business, tell him that he had failed miserably in his intentions, because she had no ideas of leaving Crete. Funny, she thought bleakly, how the decision gave her little pleasure. Somehow nothing seemed to matter any longer. If only his face wasn't always in her mind, strong and masculine and smiling, the special smile he seemed to keep just for her. The traitorous thought pierced her of his lips, his well-shaped lips seeking hers, and a cold hand seemed to close around her heart.

The thoughts crowded in. Adam was a man of substance and authority, attractive, at home in the world, a man to whom women would be instantly attracted. That was, Liz amended, if they didn't know the sneaky things he was capable of to gain his own ends. Even now she was finding it difficult to believe that everything was changed between them. But she must believe it. Somehow she had to break free from his masculine charisma.

In the end she must have fallen asleep, for she awoke to the sun's rays touching her eyelids and a dull feeling that something was wrong. Then recollection came flooding back, bringing with it the heartache there was no assuaging. She tried to gather comfort from the thought that had she gone on seeing him, revelling in the happiness of being with him, she would end up by falling in love with the man, and then where would she be? It was too late, the thought came unbidden, else why does it hurt so much to give him up? Love . . . how could she have known that it could sneak up on you and before you knew it, you were caught fast, even when the man you loved was unworthy of your affection! But it was all a fantasy, for Adam was merely acting a part for purposes of his own and she, fool that she was, had let herself be taken in by his tanned good looks and heart-knocking smile.

Listlessly she wrenched her thoughts aside to glance at the small gold travelling clock on the bureau. It was later than she had imagined and by now, she told herself, Katina would have left the villa to take up her duties at the hotel. She avoided glancing in the mirror, conscious of red-rimmed eyes, and pushing the hair back from her forehead, she slipped a cotton robe over her shoulders and went barefooted into the kitchen. An empty coffee cup was a mute reminder that Katina had long left the house. Liz wandered restlessly across the room to fill the kettle at the sink. Why, she wondered, had she never before been conscious of the emptiness of the villa, with only the pounding of the waves on the beach below to break the silence? She reached out a hand to switch on her small transistor, but today she wasn't in a mood for haunting Greek love songs. Irritatedly she silenced the radio and mixed instant coffee in a pottery mug. Anything to help her throw off the heavy sense of heartache that enveloped her like a storm cloud, on this blue and gold day.

Later in the morning she slipped a cotton shift over her bikini and picking up her woven Greek bag with its sun-cream, beach towel and tinted glasses, she made her way out of the room. Thoughts of Adam's perfidy had driven everything else from her mind, and it was with a vague sense of surprise that she picked up from beneath the front door a letter that was lying there. The next moment she ripped open the envelope, her lacklustre gaze scarcely taking in the import of the words. Kostas—it was from Kostas Baltsa the lawyer in Heraklion, who had written in reply to her enquiries. The information penetrated her disturbed senses. Regret to have to inform you . . . costs prohibitive . . . your finance not sufficient to meet cost of goods . . . As to a loan, he was sorry to inform her she was not eligible at short notice . . . a foreigner in the country . . . but he himself would be happy to oblige in order that she could start up her business . . . a short-term loan, say two years at usual interest rates . . . Will be happy to visit you in order to discuss matter . . . obtain signature to documents . . . Tuesday next unless I hear to the contrary . . . Liz thrust the letter into her bag and made her way over the sand, warm to the touch of her bare feet, past the empty taverna and down towards the beach, shimmering in the hot sunshine. Waves were whipped into a myriad sparkling points in the sea breeze, and except for a group of children playing in the shallows, the shore was empty. Soon Liz was floating on her back in the water, moving with the waves and letting the sensuous touch of the sea soothe away a little of her crashing disappointment and sense of let-down. Afterwards she splashed through a shower of white foam tumbling on the sand and spreading out her towel a little further up the shore, she dropped down. The next moment she slipped on the dark glasses that successfully concealed the evidence of reddened eyelids and traces of tears. As the time went by small groups of tourists, probably staying at Adam's hotel, made their way through the screen of pink oleanders to wander down to the shore. More than one masculine gaze rested appreciatively on the slim curves of Liz's lightly tanned young body, but, aware of the stranger's interest, she feigned sleep and before long she was once again alone.

She stayed there for a long time, watching the lazy curl of the breakers, the liquid green fire rippling along the wave to break lazily and splinter into a shower of white foam running along the wet sand.

'Hi, beach girl, remember me?' She was jerked into sudden awareness. That deep familiar voice that could make her perfectly ordinary name sound like a caress! She stiffened, summoning up all her defences as Adam, relaxed and smiling, dropped down at her side.

'Hey, take those off—I can't see you!' Before she could protest he had whipped away her sunglasses, revealing all too clearly a face blotched and swollen with weeping.

'Tears, Liz?' His smiling expression gave way to one of concern. Indeed, the thought ran through her mind, if she hadn't known better, she would have taken it for a look of downright caring! He threw an arm around her smooth shoulders. 'What's the problem, honey? Tell me, I might be able to help.'

Idiot that she was, the tenderness in his voice all but unnerved her. Swiftly she jerked herself away. 'You should know!' She expected to see guilt in his face, but instead he appeared to be genuinely puzzled.

'What are you getting at?'

'As if you didn't know!' She raised accusing eyes to his bewildered gaze. 'All this time and you didn't let on to me that you were the hotel owner who'd made a high offer for the villa and the taverna! Katina,' she choked on the word, 'told me all about it! At least she was open and above-board about wanting me to sell my share, but you—' she raised heavy eyes, then found she was unable to sustain his brilliant, *honest*-looking gaze. 'Why didn't you tell me,' she said very low, 'that you were the one who wanted to buy the place?' A wild hope stirred in her. 'It is true, isn't it?'

His tone was ice-cold. 'If you mean I knew who you were all along, that's right.'

'Then why didn't you come right out with your offer to me?'

He shrugged broad shoulders. 'What would have been the point? You didn't make any secret about hanging on to the place. I decided to let things ride for a while, especially as by then—' He broke off.

'By then—what?' And you'd better think up a good excuse, she thought.

There was an enigmatic look in his eyes. 'I guess,' despite all she now knew of him, his twisted smile all but broke through her defences, 'the way I figured it by rushing my fences I stood a good chance of losing you as well as the beach place.'

Liz threw him a disbelieving glance from under her lashes. She said very low, 'Would it matter?'

Adam rose to his feet and stood looking down at her. All at once he was remote, cold and unyielding, his lips no longer curved in a rueful smile but hard and set. *What have I done?* The thought ripped through her senses. But I had to do it!

She forced herself to say the words that must be said. 'You were determined to get around me and persuade me to sell to you, to change my mind about things,' in spite of herself she winced, 'one way or another!'

'Look,' grated Adam, 'if you want me to give it to you straight, sure, I did hope to have a shot at getting you to change your mind about selling the place—who wouldn't in my position? A friendly discussion, what's wrong with that?'

'Nothing,' she shot back, 'only you didn't say a word to me about it.' She said very low, 'Were you waiting until we—got to know each other better. Was that it?'

His eyes were ice-cold. 'Something like that.'

She threw him an accusing look. 'If only you'd told me—'

'I planned to, at the right time!'

It was just as Katina had told her, she thought on a wave of anger. All the frustration and heartache and disappointment gathered in a hard knot in her stomach and the words seemed to fall from her lips without her volition. 'It would have been easy then for you to talk me around to your way of thinking—' She broke off. The thought cut deep, because she knew it was the truth. The next moment, horrified, she realised she had betrayed her growing feeling for him. Swiftly she attempted to cover the slip. 'That's what you thought, isn't it?'

'The hell it's not!' She saw a muscle twitch in Adam's tanned cheek. There was no doubt but that she had got through to him, for plainly he was furious with her.

'If you want it straight,' he grated, 'after I met you— and "after" is the operative word—I rather valued your . . .' a momentary pause, 'friendship. I thought, hell, if I make an offer for her place she'll refuse me right off and I'll have lost out for good—'

'You'll lose out anyway,' she said with bitter irony.

His tone was steel. 'I wasn't meaning just a matter of property—forget it.' He added curtly, 'You've evidently made up your mind that the whole thing is a put-up job for the purpose of buttering you up—'

'A long-term project, wasn't that the way you put it?'

His face darkened with anger and she suspected he was holding on to his temper with an effort. 'If that's what you want to believe—'

'What else can I think?'

He was silent for a moment, the brilliant eyes raking her pale face. 'You could have a go at believing what I tell you.'

'But I did,' she flashed back at him, 'though it was more what you didn't tell me. And look,' she added bitterly, 'where that got me!'

'A bit of trust in me might help.' The words seemed to cost him an effort. 'What do you say?'

She looked across at him, unaware of the wistfulness in her gaze as she took in the lean tanned face and muscular body, the soft dark hair she'd always longed to touch. How was it that Adam could affect her so—so physically, when all the time she knew his motives were devious and calculating? She must make herself remember what he was really like, or else she was lost. It was easier to answer him, the thoughts ran through her mind, if she avoided looking at him, because that made her think him incapable of ulterior motives or deception. How could she ever trust him again? The truth is, deep in her mind a small voice spoke, that you don't trust *yourself* where Adam is concerned! She thrust the thought away and steeling herself to harden her resolve, shook her head.

'I get it,' he gritted in a low harsh tone. 'You've made up your mind that I was softening you up to put the big question?'

Liz said very low, 'What else can I think?'

'Okay!' His face was dark with anger. 'If that's the way you want it! If you're so ready to take the word of a Greek girl who has an axe to grind—'

'Haven't you?' she flared. 'You're the one who wants the whole set-up, the one whose business depends on getting it. You managed to get around Katina, that was easy—'

He said savagely. 'I had no need to "get around her", as

you put it! She's been breaking her neck to sell out from the word go—and you know it!'

It was the humiliating thought of the other two scheming together to outwit the naïve New Zealand girl that made the hot anger rise in her. Oh, she hated them both! 'I guess,' the pain-filled words came from the heart, 'that it was easy for you to fool me. At first I just couldn't believe that you would do such a thing!'

'Don't believe it now! If only you'd listen to me! Look—' he took her hands in his and for a moment the trembling in her put everything else from her mind. Swiftly he pursued his advantage. 'All right then, I did want to get you to change your mind and sell me your uncle's place. I got the idea that when we got to know each other a bit better, we could talk it over between us, come to an arrangement—'

'Get to know each other!' His touch was setting her nerves on fire, raising in her a flame of longing that threatened to take control. Wildly she gathered her thoughts together. 'Is that what you call it?'

His voice was gentle. 'Believe me, Liz, I wouldn't trick you for the world.'

She wrenched her hands from his warm clasp.

'So you say.'

If only she could believe him. If only she didn't know that the kisses that had stirred her so, sent her winging into that wild unaccustomed happiness, to him were of no importance. Oh, he might not term his caresses 'a trick', but that was what it all amounted to. To Adam his light lovemaking hadn't meant a thing, how could it? And thank heaven he would never know the way that just being with him affected her. The thought made her say stonily, 'I just wish you'd told me—'

He cut in swiftly. 'What good would that have done? You'd have brushed me off with a quick "nothing doing". Even if you'd been any girl—' quickly he caught himself up. 'What I mean is, I figured that given time to weigh up the pros and cons you'd come to realise that it was no good your hanging on to the place here, there'd be no future in it, and that's when I planned to put it to you to settle up with me over the deal!'

'Any girl?' Her mind was still puzzling over the words. 'What could he mean? Surely not that in his mind she meant something to him, even at the start? Ridiculous, in the light of what she now knew of his real nature. He must have been referring to her relationship with Jim Kay, her uncle. Aloud she said coldly, 'Too bad that I happened to have other ideas!' A betraying wobble in her voice spoiled the bravado of her words.

'That's it, then!' Adam's voice was taut with anger. And another part of her mind registered that his deep tan couldn't hide the whiteness around his lips. Strange. But of course he was upset, bitterly disappointed at losing the property he had set his heart on obtaining. Look at the way in which he had schemed to make her part with it, *one way or another*. The words tolled like a bell in her heart. How could she have allowed herself to be so easily fooled? she asked herself. The answer came unbidden. It was because she had believed in him, regarded him as a man of integrity, someone who was honest and straight—*and damned good-looking*, a tiny voice spoke in her mind. Liz thrust the thought away. It was over, over. What did the past matter now? All at once she felt drained of all emotion. Could that be her own voice, thick with unshed tears? 'It's—goodbye, then?'

He made no move to go. 'I'll make you see reason,' he muttered, 'one of these days!'

Now she had her emotions firmly in hand. 'I'll be right here,' she taunted him, 'all the time!'

'What makes you so sure?' He bent on her his deep disturbing stare.

All at once she remembered the crumpled letter in her bag. Humiliation and a fierce desire to get even with him sparked her to say triumphantly, 'I've got news for you! I've got the finance I needed to ahead with my taverna, American-style, so you won't be getting rid of me after all!'

'Good for you!' His voice was deadpan. 'You've managed to raise the cash you needed?'

'No problem at all!' Deliberately she made her tone light and carefree. 'My lawyer's lending it to me—a personal loan, so he told me in his letter. He's coming to see me about it and once it's fixed up I'll be away. I—' She stopped short, aware of his thunderous expression. 'What's wrong with it, for heaven's sake?'

'Everything!'

'I don't know what you're getting at,' she flung at him.

'Don't you?' His lips had a satirical twist.

'No, I don't!' But her heart was thudding. 'It's only a matter of business!'

'You're dead wrong if that's what you think!' She barely caught his low muttered words. 'Put him off, Liz! Tell him you've changed your mind about the loan!'

'I will not!' she flared. 'Why should I?'

His eyes were blazing. 'Can't you see what you're letting yourself in for? A man with his unenviable reputation where women are concerned? Don't you realise that asking him to lend you money puts you right in his power? He calls the tune, and it doesn't need to be a matter of hard cash when it comes to the repayment. Alone as you are here—'

Her eyes flashed angrily. 'And stupidly naïve? Isn't that what you were going to say?'

'No, it's not!' All at once the barely controlled anger she sensed in him boiled over and his hands were on her shoulders, digging into the flesh with painful pressure. 'You little fool, Liz! Can't you see what you're doing when you make a deal with a man of Kostas Baltsa's reputation?'

'You've no need to worry yourself about me!' she cried, breathing hard, 'and take your hands from my shoulders! You're hurting me!'

Immediately his hands fell away. 'Sorry—sorry about that.' She had to strain to catch the low tones, 'I wouldn't want to hurt you—not you, Liz.'

All at once she felt a wild urge towards hysteria. For clearly Adam was more concerned regarding the danger of her losing her virginity to the Greek lawyer than the matter of his setting out on the chance of acquiring the property from her. Aloud she demanded, 'Don't you think I can look after myself?' And before he could make an answer, 'Not that I need to. Honestly, the things you're suggesting about a perfectly respectable lawyer! The way you're going on about him anyone would think he was a brigand from way back in the mountains of Crete and primitive as they come!'

'He is,' Adam said harshly. 'Where women are concerned, he's earned himself a reputation all over the island as a fairly unsavoury character—cruel type.'

'Oh, you just don't like him!' she countered swiftly. 'He's been very good to me. He told me when I first arrived in Crete that I must let him know if I needed any help, and I could tell by the way he spoke that he really meant what he said!'

'I'll bet he did!' Adam's mouth was a hard line. 'When's he coming to see you?' He shot the words towards her.

'Tuesday of next week.'

'Liz,' all at once his face was dark with anger, 'will you listen to me?'

She wrinkled her nose at him. 'Not when you insist on playing the heavy father—'

He said exasperatedly, 'At least arrange to have someone else in the house with you.'

She threw him a mocking glance. 'Like you?'

Adam ignored the taunting note in her voice. 'I'd be there like a shot! Just say the word—' His voice hardened. 'Good grief, do something to protect yourself, girl!' His mouth tightened. 'Do I have to spell it out?' He looked as incensed, Liz thought in some surprise, as if the matter were of importance to him—which of course was absurd. His voice, threaded with urgency, cut across her thoughts. 'Look, Liz, do what you like. Stay on at the villa and forget about starting up the taverna again. Something might turn up. But do me a favour and don't let that guy come to the villa!' Suddenly his voice was low and persuasive. 'Come on, Liz, I happen to know what I'm talking about. Can't you take my word for it?'

His word! That did it, she thought on a spurt of anger. Weakly she had been tempted to put her trust in him all over again, even after what had happened to her owing to that very mistake in judgment. Summoning up her determination, she said stiffly, 'No, I can'! Not after the way you've let me down!'

His lips were a tight line and anger blazed in his eyes. 'Right!' He had turned away and was striding away from her. Liz stared after him as he moved swiftly over the sand. He hadn't even said, 'So long, be seeing you!' He'd just . . . gone. She blinked the stupid tears from her eyes. It was what she'd wanted, wasn't it, to show him that she refused to be dictated to by him and that his advice was wasted on her? Already she had been taken in by his force and strength and sheer male magnetism one time too many. She'd had to show him, hadn't she, that he couldn't talk away her objections, not this time.

She had certainly achieved what she had set out to do, because plainly he was furious with her. It was almost as if she had somehow hurt as well as angered him. As if he'd cared about what happened to her—but of course, she told herself a moment later, he had good reason to be angry with her. For Kostas' loan to get her started on her project would mean the end of any hopes Adam might still have of her having to sell out and leave the country. Why must she keep forgetting the real reason for his annoyance?

She had had the satisfaction of evening the score with Adam, hadn't she? She should be feeling triumphant and happy and smug. Somehow, though, there was only this dull ache in her heart and an odd sense of regret.

CHAPTER SIX

LIZ stayed on the sand, hands linked around her knees, staring over the sparkling sea with eyes that saw only Adam, walking away from her, moving out of her life. Don't think of him! Determinedly she sprang to her feet and ran down the sand to plunge into the sea, but the cool invigorating contact with the waves eased her mind only temporarily, and at last she splashed back through foaming breakers to spread her towel once more on the sand. Conscious of heartache and a vague sense of regret, today she found little pleasure in sunbathing. Fool! Forget Adam! In an effort to follow her own advice she took the Greek lawyer's letter from her bag and smoothed it out as she tried to concentrate on the typewritten words that formerly she had merely skimmed over. 'Regret not able to oblige you with loan owing to certain rules pertaining to foreigners . . .' Funny, she thought dully, she had never thought of herself as a foreigner here. 'However, as a favour I will be glad to help you by arranging a personal loan at a special low rate of interest on a two-year term. By good fortune I happen to have business to attend to in your area on Tuesday and will call and discuss arrangements with you, let us hope to our mutual advantage. Kindest regards, Kostas.'

Somehow she couldn't believe that Greek lawyers were in the habit of signing only their first names on business letters to new clients. And he was coming to see her at the villa! The niggle of unease refused to go away. Why must she recall at this moment the hot dark eyes that had raked her body mercilessly at their meeting in his office? A cold finger of apprehension touched her. Suppose Adam were right and Kostas demanded from her a higher return for his loan than she was prepared to pay? There was some-

thing about him. Beneath the suave businesslike exterior
she sensed a certain ruthlessness—primitive, male, de-
manding. The next moment she took herself in hand. She
would take Kostas' letter at its face value and curb her
over-active imagination. Immediately she spoiled the
resolution by a thought: Even if her worst fears were
realised she could cope, of course she could! It was Adam
who had put these groundless fears into her mind, she told
herself. No doubt, she mused on a sigh, he was discredit-
ing the lawyer as a part of his 'Get rid of Liz' campaign.
There she went, thinking of him again!

All at once a restlessness consumed her. She couldn't lie
in the sun any longer. Now that Adam had left her she felt
a conspicuous figure on the beach, and ignoring the
appreciative glances and shouted comments of a group of
Greek Romeos who happened to be passing by, she
wandered up the stretch of sand. Today the taverna
seemed to her to appear more than ever abandoned with
its empty tables and faded canvas awnings flapping in the
breeze. But not for long, she vowed silently. The Greek
lawyer had offered to help her (she thrust aside the
memory of his intimate glance). He would see her through
her financial problems, so she had best stop feeling sorry
for herself and get on with living. She told herself she had
had a lucky escape from falling even more deeply in love
with a man whose devious and cunning ways had almost
succeeded in deluding her.

If Katina's boasts were to be believed, the taverna had
once been a happy, noisy place, crowded with customers.
Would it be that way again, she wondered, when she had
only the plainest of fare to offer? But her clientele would be
different, she encouraged herself—guests from the big
hotel over the hill, relaxing after a swim in the sea in the
shade of the taverna or beneath sun-umbrellas set out on
the sand. It would be a huge success. Why not? And what
a triumph that would be! Then she could prove to
Adam—Resolutely she wrenched her thoughts aside,
forcing herself to concentrate on plans for the future.

Tomorrow, she promised herself, she would have a trial run, have a go at baking rolls—she had noticed a bottle of dried yeast and a bag of flour in the kitchen of the villa. How fortunate that at the last moment she had slipped into her travel pack the well-used notebook she had brought with her with its recipes she had used while flatting in Auckland. Maybe, she thought bleakly, she had been lucky too that her flatmate had loathed cooking and it was left to Liz, who enjoyed trying out new dishes, to provide the meals. And while she was counting her blessings, there was something she had to thank Adam for, she thought bleakly, one thing he had done for her, even if unwittingly. For the erection of the luxury hotel nearby, she mused, had no doubt been the means of her uncle having electricity at the villa, even though the old blackened stove remained in the kitchen.

Next morning she awoke feeling unrefreshed with a dull ache at her temples. With a heavy heart, she told herself that it was time she was up and about, she had work to do. She should count herself lucky, she told herself, being able to practise her cooking here in the villa, with nothing else to do and all the time in the world to do it. Yet somehow all her shining enthusiasm in her planned project had left her and all she could think of was Adam. Who would have believed his smiling strong face could be so cold and forbidding?

To her relief, a mug of hot coffee lifted the little hammer blows of pain in her forehead, and after she had cleared away the few dishes from her frugal breakfast, she changed her nightdress for a green and white spotted cotton frock, short and sleeveless, and coiled her hair in a careless knot on the top of her head for coolness.

Back in the kitchen she tied around her slim waist an apron she found in a drawer. It was such a small size that she suspected it had been worn by the Greek girl, and in an angry gesture she tugged it away. She wanted nothing to do with anything belonging to Katina. Not clothing, or pity or contempt. Or Adam? Now where had that absurd thought come from? she wondered. Just because the two appeared to be on friendly terms, to know each other so well ... And yet wasn't it strange that Adam hadn't blamed Katina for having betrayed his secret? Could it be that he was making certain of one part of the inheritance by cultivating the Greek girl's friendship? Even, perhaps, marriage? True, Katina had spoken of a dowry, but that was a matter arranged by parents or guardians. How neatly marriage with Katina would solve his problem— well, half of it! Liz couldn't understand why she was feeling so deeply about the matter. But it would do him no good, she told herself, for he would never succeed in persuading her to alter her mind regarding the sale.

As the day wore on the heat in the kitchen became all but unbearable, but despite the discomfort, Liz worked doggedly on. Her face was flushed and tendrils of dark hair clung damply to her forehead. The first batch of baking emerged from the oven passably successful but far short of the standard she was aiming for. She wiped a floury hand over her forehead, glistening with perspiration. She'd have to do better than this if she were to make a success of her venture. Time slipped by and now a profusion of crusty rolls was spread over bench and table top and the kitchen was filled with the aroma of freshly baked yeasty cooking.

Engrossed in her task, she was unaware of anything else until she noticed with surprise a plump dark hand encrusted with heavy gold rings, that appeared around the edge of the door. The next moment a swarthy, thickly set man wearing an immaculate business suit, stood in the opening. Kostas! He'd come a day early, she thought in confusion.

'I could not make anyone hear with the door knocker,' he was saying, 'so I let myself in. So, you are already starting to make the bread!'

Liz straightened, aware of his intimate glance that lingered on the plunging neckline of her dress. His gaze lifted to her flushed, surprised face. 'You got my letter saying I was coming to see you?'

'Yes, of course.' She was recovering her wits. 'Tomorrow. I thought you were coming tomorrow.'

He was regarding her with a fatuous smile. 'I knew you would like me to come sooner to tell you that I can help you—so here I am.'

She asked quickly, 'Have you been to the villa before?'

He shook his head. 'Your uncle, always he came to see me in my office as do all my clients—except you, Elizabeth. With you I make an exception. It is a long drive, but I do not mind. I asked at the hotel for directions.' Taking a spotless white handkerchief from his pocket, he mopped the beads of moisture on his forehead. 'It is not a day for walking over hills, but,' his warm significant glance made her feel vaguely apprehensive, 'it will be worth it all to you—and me.'

Liz said briskly, 'If I'd known you were coming today I'd have been more presentable.' All at once she was aware of long red burn marks on her hands, a scorched dress, and she suspected that she had smeared flour over her face.

'Do not worry yourself. Me, I like you this way.'

Something in his tone sent a tremor of apprehension running along her nerves. Could she handle a situation that could possibly be fraught with danger? The next moment she told herself she was being stupidly imaginative, overreacting to Kostas' intimate manner. She wrenched her mind back to his deep tones.

'In our country our women stay in the home looking after their men and the children they bear them. They work in the fields—'

'Yes, I know,' Liz tried for lightness. 'I've seen them gathering herbs and olives, working all day in the hot sun.' Nervousness made her run on breathlessly, 'And the older women, I'm not so sure they're as old as they look either, they're so burned and brown, dressed in that blacker-than-black clothing. It must be so depressing for them.'

He eyed her in astonishment and she saw with relief that she had succeeded in diverting his conversation from personal channels. 'Many of them are widows. It is only right that they should give up all attempts to please Greek men. It is the custom. They do not wish for anything else.'

'How do you know?' Liz demanded indignantly. 'How would any man know how a woman would feel about that sort of thing?'

'Ah,' with sudden misgiving she realised too late she had fallen into a trap, 'between a man and a woman, who knows the feelings?' His ingratiating smile, Liz thought, was more in the nature of a leer. 'Me, I have a feeling for you. That was why I came to see you here, to tell you you have no need to worry any more about the money. I will see that you have it. You understand, Elizabeth? You can rely on me.'

I only hope I can, Liz told herself silently. She was beginning to have mixed feelings regarding her visitor. It would be a wonderful relief to have the loan she had requested of him, but if the offer carried conditions she couldn't and wouldn't agree to in any circumstances . . . the disturbing thoughts ran through her mind.

'I'll make coffee,' she said abruptly. 'That long drive in the heat,' she heard herself babbling on, 'you must be feeling like some refreshment. I'll let you try out one of my rolls. Why don't you go into the other room,' she suggested, 'and I'll bring in a tray. It's cooler in there.' He made no move to leave the room, but remained standing motionless watching her, just watching. 'I like it here.' Once again she was disconcertingly aware of his warm glance.

To her chagrin she could feel the colour rising in her cheeks and felt a wave of thankfulness that her face was already flushed from the heat of the room. With hands that were unsteady in spite of herself she switched on the electric kettle and reached above the bench for pottery mugs hanging from their hooks.

'It's only instant,' she waffled on, spooning coffee powder from a glass jar. 'I expect you would prefer Greek?'

'It is of no importance.' His significant glance said, 'Only you are of importance to me today'. Liz, however, made a pretence of not noticing the unspoken message beamed from his dark orbs. Soon she was carrying a tray into the cool and uncluttered living room where Kostas dropped down onto a wooden chair. Liz thought wryly that even Kostas couldn't do much mischief when handling a freshly-baked roll!

As she sipped her coffee she kept up a light conversation, anything to avoid his significant words and glances. At last, however, coffee mugs were emptied and he leaned confidentially towards her. 'So now we come to business, the little matter you wrote me about.'

'It might be little to you,' said Liz with spirit, 'but it happens to be very important to me! You see, I've got this idea for serving refreshments at the taverna,' she ran on, 'tea, coffee, fruit drinks, baked rolls with fillings inside and then toasted. Plain food, but I think the Canadians and Americans and English tourists would appreciate it— anyway, it's worth a try!' She warmed to her subject. 'I'm sure I could make a go of it!' Rising to her feet, she moved to the window, looking out at the taverna on the sandy beach below. She forgot her apprehensions concerning the man seated opposite her and her eyes were dreamy. 'It looks so deserted somehow, but I could change all that, once I get a start! Actually, it doesn't need a lot doing to it, but I need a reliable toaster, a deep-freeze to store food in the heat and some glass-topped containers to display the various types of fillings.' Her eyes were alight with enthusiasm. 'I know I could make a success of it, once I get myself organised. I really thought,' she ran on, 'that I'd have enough money to get myself started. It sounded such a lot in drachmas—but it seems it's not enough, not by a long way.'

'That is true.'

Liz sighed. 'So that's why I wrote to ask you about costs

and if you could let me have a loan. I couldn't think of any
other way. Now, though, with your help I'll be able to—'
She stopped short, aware that he wasn't really listening to
what she was telling him, even though his attention was
centred on her lips, and in his smouldering gaze she
glimpsed a lambent flame, deep and dangerous.

Wildly she rushed into speech, saying the first words
that came into her head. 'Talking of tavernas, tell me, why
is it that in the villages, it's always men who sit there
playing with their blue worry beads?'

Kostas looked taken aback by the question. 'But of
course men sit all day in the taverna. The *kafenenion*, the
true Greek café, serves only Greek coffee and there men
can play cards or backgammon. Such a place is by custom
out of bounds for women, but in a *kafenenion* that is not
entirely full, she may sit outside for coffee.'

'Sit outside!' echoed Liz indignantly, 'They allow her to
do that? How very bighearted of the menfolk!'

It seemed, however, that sarcasm was wasted on Kostas. 'It is our way, and the women here, are lucky, for
when they get too old to work they get a pension from the
Government earlier than the older men.'

'Well, I think that's awful!' His amused glance took in
Liz's indignant expression. 'Do not concern yourselves
with such matters, *thespinis*, these are old customs, a part
of the life of a village.' A knowing grin. 'You are thinking
you would not like to marry a Greek man, but I tell you
that in Chania and Heraklion a man of business would not
send his wife off to work in the fields.'

Liz remembered the dark-suited men she had seen in
the city, well-dressed masculine figures with hands behind their backs as they endlessly clicked their worry
beads between their fingers. The next moment she realised that Kostas' thoughts were running along a slightly
different channel. 'A man like me.' A plump swarthy hand
covered hers.

'I should think not!' exclaimed Liz, and pulled her hand
from his moist grasp. 'But you would expect your wife to

provide a dowry? Now that to me is an awfully old-fashioned idea.'

'You do not understand our customs. It is an arrangement made by the parents of a girl who comes of marriageable age. More than one man may approach the parents of the girl. There are meetings, there are discussions, and it is arranged what she will bring to the union. In the villages her father will provide goats, cattle, a pig—'

'It's like selling the poor girl!' Liz burst out.

Kostas regarded her with the long-suffering patience of an adult dealing with a fractious child. 'He provides her with a place to live, sometimes it is a room built on to the parents' house, children—'

'Children!' She regarded him incredulously. 'You call that providing!'

He said complacently, 'It is what she wants above all else in life. A good man to look after her, a home of her own, a family—'

'And work,' she reminded him.

'In the villages, she must work,' he agreed. 'In the cities the marriage settlements are arranged in the same way, but the girl will bring drachmas or maybe property, a house, land—it is all part of the dowry.'

'Or a beach and a taverna?' Liz spoke unthinkingly, she couldn't resist the jibe.

All at once a light flared in his eyes and she knew she had made a dreadful mistake. He was a womanizer, she'd known it instinctively from the moment she had met him. She had tried to brush the feeling away, but now she wondered if she had acted rashly in appealing to him for help. He was a heavily built man with physical strength against which she would be powerless—She thrust the disquieting thoughts aside. Ridiculous to think this way. He was only her lawyer, a trifle amorous in his manner maybe, but she would just have to get used to that and stop dreaming up a dangerous situation out of nothing.

The next moment, however, she knew she had not been mistaken. He was leaning towards her, the swarthy face thrust close to hers. 'I knew when you asked me to come to you,' his tone was hoarse with passion, 'that you wanted me.'

Liz quelled the suddenly rising panic. 'I didn't ask you! You just came—'

'*You asked me to come here!*' A tide of red had risen beneath the swarthiness of his face and there was a glitter in the dark eyes. 'You agreed to my terms.'

'Interest terms,' she said faintly, knowing he wasn't even listening to her, 'interest on the money.'

He said hoarsely, 'Between a man and a woman there are other ways. Do not tell me that in your country such things are not known—'

'Yes—no—' Liz scarcely knew what she was saying. Then all at once a cold steely anger took possession of her. She would show this easily excited man who imagined because he was physically stronger than she, that he could bend her to his will. 'You listen to me! I don't want your loan! I don't want anything to do with you!' Her voice rose high and clear. 'You can keep your money, I don't want it—or you either. Just—get out of my house!'

Kostas made no move to go but remained standing, his arms folded as he gazed down at her. 'You do not tell me to go.' She caught a threatening note in his voice. 'I am the one who, how do you say it in your country, "calls the tune".' Liz saw his expression change from anger to a self-satisfied hateful smirk. 'Is it so bad for you to be my woman?'

'Yes, it is!' She flung at him. 'Get out!'

'Come, my little one—' The low voice throbbing with passion sent panic quivering along her nerves and all at once she felt very much alone and at his mercy. The next moment he lunged himself towards her and she was caught in arms that were like steel bands. His hot breath was on her face and Liz struggled fiercely in his suffocating embrace. A black tide of anger surged through her and she sank her teeth in the fleshy arm that pinned her so securely. She caught his muttered oath of pain and rage, and something else. Was it a fleeting impression of a shadow passing by the window or a desperate need that sparked her cry, born of terror and urgency, that pierced the stillness. 'Adam! Help me, Adam!'

Her assailant gave a deep triumphant laugh. 'It is no use shouting, no one will help you!' He was fumbling with unsteady hands with the strap of her sundress.

The next moment the door was flung open and Adam stood inside, his eyes blazing, his lips a hard accusing line. Never in her life, Liz thought on a breath of relief, had she been so glad to see anyone. Dazedly she watched as Adam's bronzed sinewy arm shot forward to deal a clean blow to Kostas' chin, felling the heavy man to the floor. He lay sprawled on the floor tiles, his mouth slack and eyes wide with fear. But Adam had turned to Liz, 'Tell me,' the words came on an angry breath, 'has he hurt you? Because if he has—'

'No, no, he was only trying it on.' She pulled the strap of her sundress back over her shoulder, hiding a dark bruise.

Kostas had scrambled to his feet, his hand pressed to his bleeding chin. 'It was nothing, nothing!' warily he eyed Adam. 'A lovers' quarrel! Elizabeth invited me to come here. Ask her and she will tell you—' He stopped short in the face of Adam's threatening expression.

'Get out!' Adam's tone was low and menacing and Liz suspected it was only by an effort of will he was restraining himself from dealing out further punishment to Kostas. 'Let him go!' she said on a breath. 'He's not worth worrying about!'

'You heard what Liz said,' Adam's tone was threatening, 'so get on your way while you have the chance! Fast! And take that with you!' He flung the leather briefcase towards Kostas, who snatched it up, then turned and hurried away. The next minute the slamming of a door echoed through the room.

Liz realised that Adam was eyeing her with real concern, his eyes dark and troubled. 'You're quite sure he didn't harm you?' Reaching out a hand, he traced his palm down her smooth cheek, and as always his touch started the trembling in her. For a crazy moment she forgot everything else in the world, then somehow she dragged herself back to sanity. Because she could no longer sustain his brilliant gaze she busied herself gathering up long strands of hair that had fallen loose in her struggle and coiling them in a knot at the top of her head.

'He did scare me a bit,' she acknowledged tremulously. An instinctive honesty made her add, 'You did warn me! I guess you know Kostas a whole lot better than I do. His coming here to arrange with me about the loan I wanted was just an excuse. I should have known.' She bit her lip. 'Deep down I did know really, only I wouldn't let myself admit it.'

Adam grinned and the lift of his mobile lips made her feel once again a surge of warm happiness even though she had lost all faith in him. She *must* remember about losing faith in him, even though he had chanced to arrive here at the right moment. And that was odd, her thoughts were rioting, because Kostas had planned to come here tomorrow, and anyway, after their stormy parting, she hadn't expected ever to see Adam again. 'How did you know,' she said very low, 'that I needed you?'

He laughed, a chuckle deep in his throat. 'I happen to know Kostas, and someone had to be around to show him a thing or two!'

'But you thought he was coming here tomorrow?'

'He asked for directions to the villa from the receptionist at the hotel. I was a bit late getting the message, but I did get it. Funny thing,' she caught the glimmer of amusement in his eyes, 'I was just lifting my hand to the doorbell when I could have sworn I heard someone yelling out for me.'

Liz's face went pinker . . . and pinker. Wildly she groped in her mind for a plausible excuse for the cry that had come instinctively from some deep recess in her mind. At last she said, 'I thought I heard someone coming and I was hoping it would be you!'

He raised heavy brows and tiny flames flickered in his eyes.

'Only because,' she rushed on wildly, 'I knew you were so strong and could handle him easily.' She took in his lithe tanned body, his muscular chest revealed by his cotton shirt, open to the waist. 'I mean, you're as fit as can be, and Kostas is anything but.' Adam studied her with amused interest. 'Nice try, Liz.'

'Well, anyway,' she hastened to change the subject, 'I've learned my lesson the hard way with Kostas. To think you told me that Greek men respect and look after their womenfolk, that they've got strict ideas on the subject—'

'They have! But Kostas is no more a typical Greek than a pickpocket is typically English!' He threw her an unreadable look. 'Trouble with you, Liz, is that you're so damned appealing. Didn't anyone ever tell you?'

She laughed, the warm happiness flooding through her. 'I bet you say that to all the maidens you rescue from the wicked villain!'

'Liz—' Excitement quivered along her veins and for a dizzy moment she forgot . . . forgot. Adam made an effort to take her in his arms, but with an effort she wrenched herself back to sanity. Don't let yourself be caught in that particular trap again! She summoned all her defences and said slowly, 'I'm very grateful to you for turning up here today, but it doesn't really make any difference. Things are just the same between us.'

Instantly his arms fell away. 'I get it.' There was a cutting edge to his voice.

A vague feeling of guilt niggled at her. Or could it be the hurt she saw in his eyes that pricked her conscience? There were words that must be said. She raised clear blue eyes to his ice-cold gaze. 'I just don't know how to thank you for what you did just now.'

His face was unsmiling and she thought how remote he looked all of a sudden. Zeus back on his mountain heights once more, far, far removed from ordinary mortals? She had to strain to catch the muttered words, 'You could try believing in me for a change.'

'Oh, that . . .' It was the last thing she had expected him to say. Spiritedly she took up his challenge. 'If you mean—'

'You know very well what I mean.'

To change a dangerously emotional subject Liz said quickly, 'You were right about something else too! According to what Kostas told me the amount I need to start up the taverna again my way is way beyond what I've got. That's why I'd asked him to loan me the money to get started. I guess,' she finished on a sigh, 'I can kiss all those ideas goodbye right now.'

This is the moment, she told herself, for him to make me an offer for the property, and waited for him to say the words. To her surprise, however, he appeared to have lost interest in the matter. He shrugged powerful shoulders. 'That's the way the cookie crumbles—See you!'

She could almost *feel* the emptiness of the room after he left her.

She stood motionless, the slow tears trickled down her face. She had done the right thing, the only possible thing now she knew of his real feelings towards her, so why did she feel this devastating sense of loss? Could it be because of the way he had helped her out of a desperate situation? He has his good points, she conceded, he knew I was alone here and unprotected. No doubt he would have done the same for any girl on her own. But that didn't give him the right to take up their friendly relationship once again, as though nothing had happened between them. As if she weren't aware of his true purpose to keep right on with his 'buttering up Liz' campaign. Her soft lips firmed. Because it wouldn't work—and anyway, she told herself determinedly, he won't get the chance!

The troubled thoughts chased round and round in her mind. The hurt she had glimpsed in his eyes when she had told him her feelings about him. But of course he was disappointed with her decision because of his own interest in the property. The mistake she had made, she chided herself, was in letting herself forget that despite his male charisma, his devastating smile and dark good looks, Adam was first and foremost a business man. A man who had invested the main part of his capital in a project on the coast of a Greek island in a venture that had yet to prove its popularity with the tourists arriving at Heraklion from planes and tourist ships at the start of the summer season. One factor only stood in the way of making his luxury hotel a glittering financial success, and that was an unknown girl from the other side of the world. A girl who could be as determined as himself. True, she had at first allowed herself to be taken in by Adam, but, she steeled herself, now that she knew his real reason for cultivating her friendship, she was forearmed. For a time, she admitted, she had been—well, attracted to him, but not now, not any longer.

CHAPTER SEVEN

As the next few days dragged by, Liz felt restless and unhappy. Who wouldn't, she reasoned with herself, after the crashing disappointment of having all hopes of making a new life for herself come to an end? Only when she was down on the beach, swimming in the clear water, could she dispel a little the sense of letdown, forget her problems—and Adam.

Today, as she slipped a light cotton robe over her yellow bikini and closed the door behind her, she was struck as always by the luminous quality of the light. On the sun-dappled waters a caique sailed by, but otherwise she and the seagulls crying overhead had the bay to themselves. The dolphins rising from the water far out at sea, the piercingly blue sky, it was all so beautiful, she mused as she strolled over the warm sand. A dream island. So why couldn't she just enjoy it instead of letting her mind dwell endlessly on a man who she knew full well wasn't worth a single thought? The ache of longing that spoiled even the attraction of sun and sea warned her that she was allowing Adam to take over her thoughts, her life, and she would be wise to avoid seeing him ever again—if she could.

She roused herself to plunge into the bracing, tumbling froth of the surf, then struck out for deep water. Soon she lay floating on her back, her face upturned to the clear blue bowl of the sky and her dark hair drifting like seaweed around her shoulders. She stayed in the water for a long time, then at last she splashed through the waves at the shoreline and paused to wring seawater from the thick fall of her hair. For an hour she lay sunbathing on her towel spread out on the sand, then she dusted the sand from her knees, slipped on her robe and moved away. 'I've got to organise myself into some sort of activity,' she told herself resolutely.

Anything to make her forget Adam's dark good looks and masculine attraction against which she seemed powerless. Maybe today she would take herself on a tour of Knossos, the site of the long-buried and excavated palace of the Minoans of which she had read in her guide book. She couldn't imagine herself finding much interest in three-thousand-year-old ruins, but it would be something to do. Besides, the thought came unbidden, she wouldn't be here for more than a few months, not in her present low state of finances, so she must make the most of her time and see as much of the island as she could. On the day of her arrival here she had noticed tour buses bearing the destination name of the famous place. The vehicles had made a stop at the hotel in order to pick up passengers, so evidently all she need do would be to wait there until a tour bus came along.

Presently she was back in the villa, showering the salt from her hair, finding fresh underwear and slipping into a dress of cool, creamy-coloured muslin. Copper jewellery had been her usual choice when wearing the dress, but today she would wear the gold honey-bee pendant that Adam had given her. Why not? It would be absurd to leave such an exquisite piece of jewellery here when it complemented so perfectly the low scoop of the neckline of her dress. Besides, she wanted to prove to herself that she had no emotional hang-ups about a gift from a man who despite all she knew of him, nevertheless held for her a deep and powerful attraction.

She had little appetite of late—blame that infuriating man over at the hotel—but she made herself a tomato sandwich and mixed a mug of instant coffee, then she cleared away the dishes and picked up her Greek embroidered bag. Her cheeks were flushed with the touch of the sun, making her eyes look a deep smoky blue and her damp hair clustered in tendrils around her forehead as she set off along the track. I wish I'd taken the trouble to read up the history of Knossos, she thought regretfully as she made her way up the dusty path winding between the silvery green of olive trees.

When she arrived at the concrete surround of the hotel, there appeared to be no bus in sight and, feeling a little conspicuous in this holiday atmosphere where couples strolled together in the sunshine or sat at tables under blue and white beach umbrellas, Liz moved into the shadows of a white wall.

Through the window she caught a glimpse into the reception lounge. Katina was seated at the desk and Adam was bending over her shoulder, scanning an open guest book lying on the desk. Liz was a little surprised to find Katina at the reception desk, then she remembered Adam having told her that the Greek girl sometimes filled in in the capacity of receptionist. Odd, she mused once again, that he had never blamed Katina in the slightest for letting on his sneaky intention to persuade Liz to sell him her share of the beach properties. It seemed that in his eyes the Greek girl could do no wrong. Now, seeing the two dark heads so close together, Liz was pierced by a pang of jealousy. With it came the reflection that with Katina as his wife, Adam would have no need to worry about a half share of the inheritance, that was for sure, nor would Katina have any problems about finding money for her dowry. The thought was unaccountably depressing, and Liz stared resolutely up the empty road.

She was still there ten minutes later when a voice said, 'Waiting for someone?'

She spun around, her thoughts whirling. Only one man she knew spoke in that deep vibrant tone. 'Adam!'

His eyes were glinting with an emotion she couldn't define. Amusement? Interest? Surprise? And he gave not the slightest indication of remembering his punishing kiss in the darkness of the courtyard. And that, she thought swiftly, was a game at which two could play. She pulled herself together and tried out her newest, most carefree smile. 'The bus, actually. There'll be one along for Knossos at any minute, I expect.'

'You'd be so lucky!' Diamonds of light flickered in his eyes and his mouth had the upward twist at the corners that Liz didn't quite trust. 'Knossos, you said?'

'That's right,' she answered with carefully assumed nonchalance. 'The buses were making a stop here on the day I arrived.'

'Not for you, I'm afraid.' His tone was deceptively regretful.

Liz forgot all about being carelessly unconcerned in the matter. 'Why ever not?' She stared up at him, wide-eyed. 'There is public transport, isn't there?'

'Sure, but it happens to be excursion buses, all booked up by travel agents for overseas tourists. To get public ones you'd have to start from scratch from Heraklion—'

'Oh!' He was looking amused once again and hurriedly Liz said, 'I'll order a taxi, then. If I could ring for one from the office?'

'No need, you've got yourself one right now!' There was a dancing light in his eyes and he appeared to be enjoying himself hugely, she thought. Could this be a further attempt at friendly persuasion? Aloud she queried, 'With you, you mean?'

'Why not? The old bus is ready and waiting!' He jerked a hand towards the gleaming red car standing in the garages nearby.

She hesitated, her thoughts spinning wildly. Just being with him sent her spirits soaring excitedly. Clearly he had decided to ignore the circumstances of their last parting. Or had he already forgotten? She brought her mind back to his deep vibrant tones. 'Everyone who comes to Crete should see the old Minoan palace,' he told her with a grin. 'And now that you—'

'Haven't much time left? Is that what you were going to say?' she flashed. Somehow he sparked her to anger, and she suspected he did it deliberately.

'Not really,' his eyes had a veiled expression. Then all at

once he was friendly. 'Come on, Liz,' his voice was low and persuasive, 'let me take you on a personal sightseeing tour. Greek mythology a speciality!' And as she hesitated. 'You'll have to have somewhere to go now that you're all dressed up—honey-bee pendant and all!'

So he had noticed the gold pendant. She threw him a suspicious look, a look, she realised the next minute, that was entirely wasted, for he merely turned away, throwing over his shoulder, 'Right! We're on our way!'

She might as well take up his offer, she reflected as she watched him move towards the car park. What harm could it do to go with him?

Plenty, piped up the small voice deep in her mind, but she thrust it aside. Just an hour or so spent rambling around the ancient courtyards and palace rooms, she reasoned with herself; she'd be foolish to refuse the invitation.

'Hop in, Liz!' Adam was pulling up at her side, leaning from his seat at the wheel of the red car to fling open the side door.

What else could she do? she asked herself as she slid into the passenger seat and he moved around the car to close the door. Clearly it was an opportunity not to be missed. But deep down where it counted she knew she really had no choice in the matter, not when Adam eyed her with his glinting eyes and heart-knocking smile!

He slipped the car into gear and as they took a rise then sped along a road cut between the thyme-scented hills, she forgot everything else in the world but Adam, his bronzed profile and his well-shaped hands on the steering wheel.

His deep tones broke the silence. 'With a bit of luck we'll get to Knossos before the main tour buses for the day show up and I can take you around without tourists getting in the way.'

'Is the palace very big?'

'Is it ever? The palace had a thousand rooms in its heyday—that's how it got its reputation as a labyrinth, and would you believe, the frescoes are almost as vivid as

the day they were created and the plumbing still works!'
They had swung into a dusty road winding between
sparsely growing olive trees and from somewhere far away
Liz caught the faint echoes of a flute.

'Pan pipes,' Adam told her. 'Some lonely shepherd way
down in the valley who's keeping an eye on his sheep.'

'I like the sound.' Liz thought she would always remember the haunting thread of music borne on the fresh,
herb-scented breeze. The sound was almost as fascinating, she mused, as the warm tones of Adam's voice as he
described to her a race who had been far ahead of their
time and had lived thousands of years ago on this island.
Funny, she had tried to study a book of Crete legends
before coming here, but it had failed to hold her interest,
yet Adam seemed to be able to communicate to her
something of his own enthusiasm for the past. She
couldn't seem to wrench her gaze from his face, and for
something to say, she commented, 'You seem to know the
palace ruins well!'

'I should do!' She took pleasure in his quick, sideways
grin. 'As a kid back in England I was brought up on Greek
myths and pagan gods—my dad saw to that! Every
summer we spent a holiday on one of the Greek islands
and I was taken to every museum in the place. Not that I
appreciated the outings much at that time, but now . . .
The odd thing about the history of Crete is that it gets you
once you start delving into it. They were quite a race, the
Minoans, good-looking and lively and graceful, and there
was nothing stuffy or pompous about their court. Judging
by the pictures and frescoes in the palace rooms they were
a happy people. They loved to dance and loved life and
built their court with lots of corridors open to the sky.
Their paintings are really something, and their stylised
gold jewellery could have been fashioned by a leading
jeweller of today.'

'Tell me,' said Liz, 'what were the women like, the court
ladies?'

'The court ladies?' He flicked her a sideways glance and

at something in his expression, her spirits soared. Stupid of her to feel this way. She wrenched her mind back to his words.

'Like you, actually. You see pictures of them on frescoes in the Throne Room of the Palace. Slim, dark, sensitive-looking with slender waists and dark curly hair. Only they didn't have your eyes. No one else could have eyes like you!'

She threw him an enquiring look and could have sworn that he really had meant what he had said about her. Maybe he did feel something for her, who could tell? She turned her face aside to hide her burning cheeks and stared out at the piles of rubble beside the road showing the danger of rock falls, as they swung around a hairpin bend. 'You're having me on.'

He said softly, 'Would I do that to you, Liz?'

A loaded question and one to which she knew the answer only too well. 'Well . . .' she let the word drift into silence and was relieved when they turned another bend in the road and Adam braked to a stop just in time to avoid the sheep that were meandering along the highway in the care of a shepherd.

'Just a matter of being patient,' Adam was leaning back in his seat. 'You don't mind a bit of a wait, do you?'

I don't mind anything when I'm with you, Adam. Now where, she wondered, had that thought come from?

'The shepherd's probably bound for a farm farther down the road.' She followed his gaze to a hillside where dark-garbed Cretan women with donkeys were gathering herbs amongst the blood-red poppies and yellow daisies growing amongst the grass. 'They certainly make the most of their herbs growing on the island,' she observed.

He nodded. 'Use them too. A Cretan woman's kitchen always has mint for indigestion and a good supply of origani to give her Greek dishes a lift.'

'Really?' She eyed him wonderingly. 'How about the dittany I can smell on the air right now?'

'Oh, that's the most important of the lot.' He threw his

arm lightly around her shoulders. 'It's said to have ther-
apeutic qualities for women in childbirth.'

Liz, however, had forgotten her question. Thank
heaven, she thought through rioting senses, Adam
couldn't know the effect his touch was having on her. The
scattered sheep were still moving around the car, and to
break the moment of silence she said, 'That peasant over
there working in his field—he surely can't expect to make
much of a living, with his primitive wooden plough.'

Adam's arm tightened around her shoulders and she
found herself blissfully relaxing against him, only half
aware of what he was saying. 'More likely he's hoping for
a much more lucrative harvest, real treasure that the
plough might turn up in the earth anywhere any time, if
he's lucky! And there's always a chance—'

She roused herself to look at him incredulously. 'You
don't mean buried treasure! Not these days!'

'You're in Crete now, Liz, and it's happening all the
time—one of the big draws of archaeology, I guess. Every
day new sites and priceless finds are being unearthed all
over the island. Take the original version of the honey-bee
pendant you're wearing,' gently he put out a hand and
lifted the fine gold wire hanging with shining discs, that
was strung around her slender throat. For a long moment
she was tinglingly aware of his hand on her skin and
fought a wild impulse to hold his hand there, close and
warm and exciting. Over the confusion of her senses she
made an effort to concentrate on his voice. His matter-of-
fact tones calmed her tumultuous thoughts. 'It was discovered in a burial ground, a royal one that had been
untouched for centuries.' All at once his tone was warm
and intimate. 'So you like your Minoan pendant?'

'Oh, I do! I do! It's the loveliest piece of jewellery I've
ever owned!' Too late she realised the excited enthusiasm
of her tone. Would he imagine that she cherished the
pendant because of the giver? She added on a breath, 'It
suits my dress.'

'And your suntanned throat.'

Liz was almost sorry to see the last sheep zigzagging its way past the car to join its woolly companions, and the next moment Adam put a hand to the starter motor.

Presently they were moving up a slope where sunlight made a filtered pattern through grapevines and ahead on high land surrounded by hills was the rambling site of the long-buried and excavated Minoan palace. Adam guided the car into a parking area, then escorted Liz through the entrance gates. While he paused to purchase admission tickets at a counter, she stood looking around her, struck by the silence and peacefulness of the place. Could this be what Adam had referred to when he had spoken of being free of the tour buses with their guides and chattering passengers? In the soft bright sunlight she caught glimpses of immense walls of stone, secluded shady courtyards, and everywhere light flooded the ruins of the palace, streaming down through open stairways and lightwells.

'You've got yourself a tour guide.' Adam had come to join her. Taking her arm, he led her up a path winding amongst tall grass and wild corn, to emerge amongst grey, time-worn stones. As she gazed over the dark red columns of high walls half buried in weeds Liz said wonderingly, 'Is the palace just as it was thousands of years ago?'

He stood at her side, following her gaze. 'More or less. When it was first discovered and excavated, the thousand-years-old sunbaked bricks couldn't take the daylight, so the palace and courtyard buildings were reconstructed—red pillars, stone walls, the lot. Right here is the central courtyard,' he led the way over silvery-grey stones half covered in encroaching weeds. 'If you stand here beside me,' he drew her to him and she was aware once again of the thrilling awareness his touch evoked, so that she had to force herself to concentrate on his words, 'from here the courtyard frames a view of Mount Jouktas.'

At last she had her runaway emotions in hand. 'Isn't that the sacred mountain, home of the Earth Goddess, the mother of all living creatures?'

'You've been boning up on Cretan mythology!'

'Not enough. I never thought it was interesting until now.' She broke off. Fool! she scolded herself, you can't speak without betraying yourself! Hurriedly she attempted to rectify the blunder. 'Only because I like that bit about the Minoans worshipping the Earth Goddess!' She twinkled up at him. 'It appeals to me much more than the modern Greek idea of the womenfolk getting dried-up skins and old-looking working in the fields in the hot sun while the men sit around in the taverna and play with their worry beads. Yet the Minoans lived so long ago.'

'They were way ahead of any other civilisation of their time—Come on, I'll take you down to the cellars and storehouses.'

They moved beneath the clear dazzling light above, down wide stone steps with black inverted columns, to make their way along low passageways and past great red columns, then down a staircase into the old cellars.

'I don't believe it!' Liz started in amazement at great seven-foot-high pottery jars with their ornate decorations of coloured scenes. 'They could have come right out of a stage production of Ali Baba and the Forty Thieves!'

The air was cool in the dim passageways as they wandered through workshops and storehouses, all arranged around the great Central Court. Liz looked with amazement at the Queen's toilet with its incredibly modern fitments, the luxurious bathroom with its red clay tub. Then they climbed a stone stairway to stroll out on to sun-splashed terraces and through royal suites with their exquisitely decorated rooms in this palace open to the sky.

'Now for the Throne Room.' Adam took her up some steps to the restored room with its gypsum throne and guardian griffons.

'It's not a bit like the throne room I'd pictured.' In the room flooded with light from the opening above, Liz took in the richly glowing colours of frescoes depicting the court ladies in their topless, long-skirted gowns, their dark hair curling in ringlets around their delicate faces. Murals showed the bare-breasted Snake Goddess, and everywhere on doorways and walls was the sacred symbol, she had come to know all over Crete, the double axe and the bull's horns. 'It's beautiful!' Her eyes were alight. 'What did you say it was called, this palace? The Palace of the Double Axe? Anyone can see that the folk who lived in the court here were a happy people who loved beauty. You've only got to look at the frescoes and the hairstyles and jewellery of the women.' Once again Liz's gaze was drawn to the frescoes with their pictures of tiny, delicately featured people who looked full of gaiety and charm. 'Can't you just see them moving about the shady courtyards and enjoying themselves on the dancing floor? And the throne—it's more like an ordinary dining chair of today. So simple, and so little.'

Adam was leaning lazily against a pillar, regarding her with speculative grey eyes. 'Big enough for you.'

She twinkled back at him. 'King Minos must have been a very small person. I don't think I—'

'Want to bet?' Before she could argue the matter he had scooped her up in his arms, then gently he seated her on the tiny throne.

The next moment an echo of voices warned them of the approach of a tour party. Swiftly Liz sprang to her feet, Adam grasped her hand and like conspirators, laughingly they made their escape. Presently they came out into the hot sunshine of a sun-drenched terrace, to wander down a curving path and drop down to stones half hidden in a riot of golden daisies. It was very still, the only sound the droning of bees in air that was heavy with the perfume of trailing honeysuckle. A short distance away groups of tourists were moving towards the ticket booth, milling amongst the stone stairways of the palace rooms and wandering through the souvenir store. Yet here she and Adam were alone in a secluded spot where corn grew high amongst the flagstones and scarlet poppies flamed between great silvery-grey stones half hidden in encroaching weeds.

'I can see why you said those Minoan people were way

ahead of other civilisations of their time.' Liz spoke
dreamily with one half of her mind. Her gaze was fixed on
Adam's dark, lean face. He was gazing out towards the
surrounding hills and she took her fill of looking at him . . .
just looking. His sensitively shaped hands and suntanned
throat, the thatch of dark hair falling over his bronzed
forehead—everything about him drew her to him, and to
be alone here with him was a happiness beyond belief. She
pulled her thoughts up with a jerk, aghast at the direction
in which they were drifting, and attempted to concentrate
on his voice. What was he saying, something about the
Minoans?

'You have to hand it to a race where just for fun, the
girls and boys took on a sport of bull-jumping, a ritual
leaping over the horns of a charging bull!'

At last she had herself in control. 'They couldn't!' Her
eyes widened. 'Or could they?'

'All the time! The thing was to face the charging bull,
then take a firm grip on the lowered horns and be flung up
in the air as the bull tossed. The trick was then to let go of
the horns, do a somersault up on to the bull's back and
take a flying leap down before it could swerve to charge
again!'

'Wow-ee! If that wasn't split-second timing—' She
added thoughtfully, 'They seemed very concerned with
the ritual thing, especially the symbol of the bull's horns
and the double axe.'

He nodded. 'One of the Cretan myths. Seems that
Queen Pasiphaë had an unnatural passion for the bulls
sacred to Knossos, especially the white ones, because the
Priest King Minos was a creature from a dynasty that had
a sky bull for its emblem—am I boring you?'

You could never bore me, Adam. Aloud she said, 'Tell me
more. It's fascinating.'

'Right, you've asked for it! Anyway, it seems the Queen
produced this bull creature, half man, half bull, and he
had to be hidden away in the palace and King Minos
persuaded the gods to agree to his demand that once a

year, seven boys and seven girls should be sent from Athens to Crete, to be thrown to the Minotaur.'

'Gruesome! What happened to him in the end?'

'Theseus—he was the son of the king of Athens—took pity on the victims and offered to go to Crete himself to kill the monster and put an end to the human sacrifices.'

'Good for him! How did he do that?'

'No problem. It seems that Ariadne, the daughter of King Minos, fell in love with the young man and showed him how to overcome the Minotaur by getting at him through his weakest point. She was right on the ball, handed him a big reel of thread which he was to unwind as he made his way through the corridors of the labyrinth. So after he had felled the monster with a single blow he followed the thread Ariadne had given him and found his way back again. Then he took the young people he'd saved, picked up Ariadne, and left for Athens.'

'Golly,' said Liz, 'that's an exciting story, especially the bit about the Minotaur! Poor old thing, I feel quite sorry for him, locked away for years in a gloomy labyrinth because he was so repulsive-looking. Just as well,' she laughed, 'that it wasn't a true story.'

Adam said slowly. 'It could be. My dad was a great one for doing research on the Greek myths and legends, and he came across a theory that the Minotaur story could be based on real facts.'

She stared at him incredulously. 'No! It couldn't be—'

'Oh, not on the face of it, but you'd be surprised how many of these old legends turn out to be real life happenings disguised in story form so as not to be recognised.'

'Like the old English nursery rhymes,' Liz said, 'that were composed by people who didn't dare come right out and say what they knew of the court people, so they made up rhymes for children to disguise the truth. But the Minotaur story—no, I couldn't go along with that being the real thing.'

'It's just a theory, Liz, but it's got something going for it all the same. Can you picture the scene right here in the palace grounds?' His tone was tinged with enthusiasm. 'It's the night of a great religious ceremony. There's chanting to their adored god Zeus and ritual dancing to the Life Goddess under a Cretan moon. Much, much later that night the religious fervour mounts to a climax and men and women put on their bulls head masks for the ceremonial marriage dance. Suppose, just suppose, Liz, that the Priest King danced, and not only danced with the Moon Priestess, what then?'

A bird's song sounded loud in the stillness and Liz had an eerie sensation of being back in a pagan past. She shook away the impression. 'I'll stick with my myth,' she said.

They wandered down an overgrown path, passing broken stone walls, and when they came in sight of the souvenir store Adam said, 'Let me get you some worry beads. And how about some postcards to send home?'

She flashed him a defiant smile. 'But Crete is my home!' At least, she told herself, I've let him know that I'm not giving up without a struggle. As he made no comment she said, 'It's a thought, all the same, especially the postcards. I've got a girl friend back in Auckland who's interested in pottery. She's got her own kiln in her backyard, and a picture of those monstrous Ali Baba jars would really make her day. I know she'd never believe the size of them otherwise.'

'And what would you like, Liz? Something to take back from Knossos is a must, you know. Let me—'

This time her smile was the real thing, warm and happy. 'Only if it doesn't cost the earth.' She had a suspicion that the honey-bee pendant she was wearing was far from that category.

'Right! You choose!' They strolled around the display shelves with their replicas of Greek urns, charms to keep away the evil spirits and hand-embroidered bags and muslin blouses. Liz picked up a tiny exquisitely fashioned lyre and plucked the miniature strings. 'Listen,' she said delightedly, 'it really plays!' As with all the souvenirs she had seen in Greece, the articles were of tasteful design and high quality workmanship. At last she selected a ceramic tile picture depicting a cluster of white cottages tumbling down to a sapphire sea, a cobbled street, a donkey. Adam paid the trifling cost of the gift and Liz placed it in her embroidered Greek bag. All at once she was filled with a feeling of high elation born of the unfamiliar surroundings, the golden sunshiny day and, why not admit it, being here with Adam. Why not forget, just for today, that there were problems between them, no reason why they couldn't be happy together as friends, even perhaps—lovers?

The thought was intoxicating. Time slipped swiftly by, and it was with a feeling of regret that Liz got into the car for the homeward journey. As they took the winding road over the hills she mused that she wouldn't mind one little bit if a group of straggling sheep once again delayed their progress. All too quickly, however, they sped over slopes with their sparsely growing olive trees, and past the fields where women herb-gatherers still worked beneath the scorching rays of the sun. Then Adam was drawing up at the hotel. He got out of the car and came around the vehicle to open the passenger door. 'I'll see you home—'

'Really,' she protested, 'there's no need!' *Liar! You're longing for him to stay with you until the last possible moment.*

'It's no use arguing with me, Liz. Haven't you discovered that yet?' As they took the dusty white goat track over the slope he clasped her hand in his, and once again Liz felt her heart lift on a great surge of pleasure. When they reached the shady secluded courtyard she hesitated, looking up at him. 'Coffee? It would only take me a minute to make it.'

'Thanks, no. I've got a man turning up for an appointment—a builder I've got to see about some alterations and extensions I'm planning to the place.'

'Oh!' There was a cold feeling inside her and her wild happiness fell away. How could she have forgotten the reason Adam had insisted on taking her to Knossos, had given such a good pretence of being happy with her? The

builder, she thought, a subtle reminder of what he really
wanted out of their association. 'If you're depending on
me to help you there,' the hot words were out before she
could stop them, 'the answer is still "no" so it's no use
your trying to get around me!'

The next moment she thought with horror, Why did I
throw the words at him like that? But she had to tell him,
didn't she? The silence seemed to last for ever.

'I get it!' His tone was steel. 'You've made up your mind
about me and there's no way I can talk some sense into
you.'

'No, there isn't!' If only her voice didn't have that
betraying wobble.

'Why not have a shot at believing in me for a change?'
The curt words flicked her raw nerves like a whip. 'You
might be surprised! No?' He clasped her roughly to him
and for a tense moment she imagined he was about to
shake her, for his hands were holding her like steel bands.
'Seeing you're so determined—' he said harshly, and
rammed home the words with a hard, punishing kiss.
Then abruptly he released her and before she could catch
her breath he had swung around on his heel and was
striding away.

Liz watched him go, her eyes blinded with unshed
tears. Stupid! Stupid! Now she had spoiled everything!
Why was she trembling like this? Just because she had
sent him away? She put a hand to her bruised lips. She'd
had to let him know that she wasn't to be so easily taken
in, hadn't she? Was it Adam or yourself that you were
trying to impress? the small voice deep in her mind
queried and she thrust it aside. A cold feeling of desolation
was spreading through her and scarcely knowing she was
moving, she went on leaden feet to the carved wooden
door and let herself inside the villa.

That night she lay wakeful, tossing from side to side in
her bed through the hot hours, thinking . . . remembering.
She had been so happy with Adam today, so terribly
happy that it had been all too easy to lose sight of the real

purpose behind his easy friendliness. Maybe, though, he did like her just a little, for herself? Could that be the explanation for his bitter anger at the resentful words she had flung at him? The reason for his punishing kiss? For when you came right down to it, he no longer had any urgent need to employ his tactics of makebelieve love making where she was concerned. He would know only too well that faced as she now was with slender resources and no way of making a living here, soon she would be forced to call it a day, to sell up her beloved Cretan inheritance and return to New Zealand. Why hadn't she realised this before? He had only to wait, or so he would imagine, until she was forced to surrender. To him! After all her fine speeches to the contrary, her misplaced confidence in the future. Never!

CHAPTER EIGHT

Somehow Liz managed to get through the following few days. Outside the sky was the same piercing blue, the seawater as warm and caressing as ever, but the radiant sparkle of her Crete holiday had lost a little of its lustre. Blame Adam, she told herself, and added the next moment, myself rather for being so stupidly vulnerable to the sheer male attraction of the man!

In an effort to dispel her heavy thoughts she went from room to room in the villa, sweeping and dusting and cleaning—but really, she decided, it was all a waste of effort. For whatever Katina's failings, her jealousy and resentment and swift emotional outbursts, there was no doubt that in line with the reputation of all Greek women, she had kept her dwelling in immaculate condition.

Today as she wandered listlessly over the sand, warm to the touch of her bare feet, Liz's gaze moved instinctively to the deserted taverna. *Her* taverna, she reminded herself, even if it was not in operation—yet. But it would be some time in the future. 'With your state of finances?' a small voice jeered in her mind. 'You're fooling yourself!' It was the truth, she admitted on a sigh. Last night she had spent a long time with ballpoint pen and paper, working out her living costs and allowing for expenses such as souvenirs she must buy for friends at home as well as tours she might want to take to places of interest. For somehow, she tried to rally herself, she must make herself forget Adam, rouse herself to take an interest in this island so rich in mythology. It all added up to the inescapable conclusion that all the money she had in the world consisted of the amount of her return fare to New Zealand plus a small sum that with luck would cover living costs for a month or so longer. A feeling of bravado made her decide to live on her capital, such as it was, for as long as her funds would let her. After that—well, she would worry about that when the time came. One thing was for sure, and that was that never would she surrender her precious inheritance to Adam. After all her fine speeches, her misplaced confidence in the future? Not this girl! She set her soft lips firmly. She wasn't beaten yet, not by a long way. She still had some time left, and by the end of summer . . .

Opening the door of the taverna, she stood looking around the big room facing the sea. Strangely she felt no sense of emptiness but rather gained the odd impression that the room was waiting for her to put her plans into action. Her plans . . . Across the screen of her mind flickered pictures where groups of laughing, happy tourists strolled over the sand to swim in the azure sea, sunbathing on the sand before making their way up to the taverna with its tables and blue and white sun-umbrellas, for welcome refreshments.

The worrying thoughts crowded back to mind. She could no longer hope for any financial help from Kostas, she had already written off that possibility. What *could* she do to solve her problem? Even the Delphic Oracle couldn't answer that one, she thought wryly. But there was no sense in negative thinking. She must take herself in hand, forget Adam and his compelling attraction for her, and concentrate on something constructive. The sooner she started doing something about it the better!

Back in the villa she decided that a swim in the bay was the best way she knew of taking her mind from problems, so she threw off her clothes and pulled on her bikini, still damp from the previous day's dip in the sparkling sea.

She found sunglasses, sun-lotion and a towel and stuffed them into her embroidered Greek bag. Then idly she picked up a paperback that she had brought with her to read on the plane trip from New Zealand. Somehow she hadn't yet got around to reading the romance written by a popular author. She leafed through the pages, then threw the book aside. Today romantic interludes were the last thing she wanted to read about—especially, the thought came unbidden, when the cover picture depicted a hero who looked a lot like Adam, though not half so devastatingly attractive. She brought her traitorous thoughts up with a jerk. Attractive—and untrustworthy, she reminded herself. Don't forget that, my girl, or you're really in for trouble! She tossed down the paperback and went into the kitchen and soon she was placing in her bag a bottle of fruit drink, bread and some *feta*, the crumbly goat's cheese she was beginning to get a taste for. As she moved through the sun-splashed courtyard she plucked a cluster of white grapes from the trailing vines, then made her way down to the beach.

On the sun-dappled waters two young men, recent arrivals in Greece she thought, judging by their pallid skins, sailed by in windsurfers, their attention, thank goodness, fully taken up with navigating their craft over the tossing waves. A middle-aged couple, obviously from the nearby tourist hotel, approached through the screen of oleander blossoms and a girl with long blonde hair and a young man in a T-shirt and jeans, arms entwined, wandered along the water's edge, oblivious of everything except each other. Liz was thankful that the bay as usual was almost empty of holidaymakers, for a pretty girl on her own seemed to invite company. Just to be sure of privacy she decided she would explore the rocks at the far end of the bay, find a spot where she could sunbathe and laze away the hours. *And think of Adam.* She thrust the thought away.

For a long time she wandered along the shoreline, splashing through wavelets until at last she stumbled on a strip of sand that ran up between high rocks. In the sheltered spot, water lapped around the rocks leaving sunlit pools where sea-creatures scuttled about their business. Far out at sea she glimpsed the glistening curves of dolphins that were lost the next minute amongst the waves. It was very still, the only sound the crying of gulls

wheeling high in the translucent blue above and the
endless murmur of turning breakers.

Lazily she let the hours slip by. Again and again she
climbed over the rocks and made her way down to the
tossing sea, swimming and floating on her back, to splash
back through the waves, enjoying the touch of salt water
on her sunwarmed skin. Then at last she threw herself
down on the sand, letting the sun have its way with her as
it sparked lights in her drying hair and soothed away the
sense of heartache and letdown. At some time during the
afternoon she must have fallen into a doze, because when
she awoke the sun was low on the horizon, the bays along
the coast lost in a shadowy sea-haze. A fishing boat,
sponges festooned over deck and rigging, cut across the
golden pathway of the setting sun—no doubt, she
thought, heading for the port of Heraklion after a day's
sponge fishing. Heavens!—dazedly she stared down at the
wrist-watch she had fished from her bag—she must have
been asleep for hours!

Shaking the sand from her towel, she gathered up her
bag and made her way back over the rocks. Soon she was
strolling along the beach, splashing along at the edge of
the waves while the fresh wind tossed her hair back
behind her ears.

As she neared the taverna, the familiar thoughts surfaced. If only she could just get herself started! She paused
on the shadowed sand. She remembered having closed the
door opening in to the living quarters of the building, yet
here it was swinging open!

Cautiously she pushed the door further open and stepped inside. Nothing wrong here. Overcoming a feeling of
trepidation, she moved into the kitchen with its wide
opening and counter. The next minute she stood still,
rooted to the spot in amazement. It couldn't possibly be
true—but it was! For fitted neatly into place at one end of
the room was a spacious deep-freeze cabinet. At the end of
the counter stood a cabinet filled with glass compartments, just waiting to be filled with delectable foods for

serving with toasted rolls. At the other end of the counter stood an electric toasting unit. Liz blinked. There was even a big new jar of Nescafé and at its side a capacious glass container filled with orange and lemon juice. Oh, this was quite unbelievable! Swiftly she glanced around the room in search of a docket, but she could find no paper of any sort.

Kostas, she mused. It must be Kostas who was responsible for all this. Only he knew of the dimensions of the stock she required to start up her venture. No doubt, she reflected, the lawyer had decided that helping her out of her financial difficulties would be a small price to pay when it came to forfeiting his own good reputation. No doubt he was feeling apprehensive that Adam, the owner-manager of surely the most impressive tourist hotel in the island, would not keep secret the matter of Kostas having taken advantage of an unprotected woman from another country, and had endeavoured to force his unwelcome attentions on her. She shuddered at the narrow escape she had had from Kostas' advances—something, she admitted to herself, for which she had to be grateful to Adam. It was lucky for her that he had chanced to be here at the moment when she most needed him. 'Lucky?' jeered a voice deep in her mind. 'He knew you were in danger from that amorous lawyer, he tried to warn you about Kostas, but you refused to listen! Adam was protecting you, that's what! Adam . . . Her soft lips drooped wistfully. If only he didn't hold this overpowering attraction for her! With an effort she jerked her thoughts aside.

But all this meant—the chill thought came unbidden—that she would find herself in Kostas' debt and suppose he came here to see her once again? This time she could expect no help from Adam. She let out a sigh of relief. But Kostas wouldn't dare, not a second time! Anyway, there would be time enough to worry about the loan when she received his letter in the mail detailing the terms of the agreement, as no doubt she would within a few days. Although she wanted no favours from his hands, she could scarcely send the goods back, since she had no idea where they had come from. All at once her spirits lifted on a wave of excitement. Wouldn't Adam be amazed when she let him know that despite his dire warnings on the subject, she now had a chance of making her own way and following her beloved project through to success after all. She couldn't *wait* to tell him that she was no longer in a position of being forced to surrender her property to him—well, she conceded reluctantly, it's half mine. Definitely, she told herself jubilantly, things were looking up!

She pressed a switch on the deep-freeze cabinet and a tiny red light flashed on. How fortunate she was that electricity was already wired to both villa and taverna— thanks to Adam and the luxury hotel he had had erected on the lonely coast.

She was looking forward already to her moment of triumph when she could tell him that his chances of acquiring the beach properties were now slimmer than ever. Not that he would seek her out again, or she him, but there might be a chance meeting. They lived not far apart, so who knew, they might run into each other. If not, she could always invent an excuse to see him—she would think of something. The prospect was exhilarating. She promised herself that tomorrow she would take a bus trip to the nearest village and visit the market there in search of fresh vegetables, eggs and fish for roll fillings.

Next day she was up early. When she had showered she dressed in the briefest of undergarments and pulled on a crisp sea-green cotton shirtwaister. Seated in front of the mirror she experimented with her hair, drawing it severely back from her forehead and catching it in a burnished knot at the back of her head. There! She looked as businesslike as she could, but it was difficult with unruly curly hair that insisted on flying out in tendrils around her face, not to mention a short, cheeky little nose.

At that moment a sound from the ornately carved door knocker brought her to the entrance, and she opened the door to face a brigand-looking Greek with a villainous moustache, wide trousers and black knee-boots. At his side stood a Greek woman wearing black garments, a dark coif shading the lower part of her sun-dried brown face. But the eyes Liz thought were shrewd and kindly.

'*Kalispéra!*' Liz uttered one of the few Greek words she knew. 'Come in.'

Smiling broadly, the couple stepped inside and immediately they broke into a spate of Greek, accompanied by excited gesticulations. Bewilderedly, Liz caught two names, Xenia and Nikos. As the flow of words went on, suddenly her uncle's name registered on her mind. 'Wait!'—She hurried from the room and returned with her uncle's photograph. The reaction was immediate. Beaming smiles and excited nods made Liz realise that at least these two people had known her uncle. All at once something clicked in her mind. Were they the married couple who had once lived here and worked with Katina in the taverna?

'Taverna?' she said enquiringly and the strangers beamed with delight. 'You used to work in the taverna here?'

It was clear to Liz, however, that only the familiar word had registered with them. If only she had taken the trouble to learn something of the Greek language! She threw up her hands, palm uppermost, and the gesture of helplessness had the effect of making the strangers talk volubly in their own language. The next minute they turned and hurried out of the door, and Liz, watching from the window, saw them approach a decrepit-looking car that stood in the driveway. After a short conversation with the driver, the three came hurrying back to the villa. And pray heaven Liz thought, that the driver can speak some English.

It seemed that he did. The driver's name was Spiro, that much she understood. A greek youth with lively dark eyes and excitable manner, he got through to Liz with the aid of much gesticulating that the middle-aged couple had heard of Liz having taken over the property and had come in the hope that they could return to the living quarters of the taverna and help with the work when the place was once again open to the public. Liz's uncle, it seemed, had promised them the use of the rooms indefinitely and only an unexpected visit to a sick relative at a village on the other side of the island had kept them away so long.

With the help of the interpreter, Liz managed to let them know that they were welcome to the use of the rooms. That she would be glad of their help in the taverna as she would soon be starting up again in business. The only thing was, she would not be serving Greek food.

The last statement brought unbelieving looks and endless explanations, but at last Liz got through to them what she meant. All at once a thought struck her. Katina? The Greek girl did, after all, have some say in arrangements, although Liz hated to admit it. She appealed to the Greek youth. 'Ask them if Katina will agree to their staying here again.'

A vigorous nodding of dark heads and a flood of excited talk made Liz realise that clearly with Katina, there was no problem at all.

'Tell them,' Liz appealed to the youth, 'that they must bring in their bags. That they are very welcome to stay for as long as they like in the taverna, just as when my uncle was here.'

The message, when passed on, brought satisfied smiles and nods, then a wild spate of Greek. It took some time for Liz to understand the import of what the strangers were saying but at last she gathered that they had asked their friend Spiro to take them in his car to the village where they could buy fresh food at the market for the taverna. Could Liz come with them and choose the freshest lettuces and peppers? It was best to be early.

'Fine!' Now it was Liz's turn to show surprise and pleasure.

'Will you tell them,' she appealed to Spiro, 'that I'm ready to go right now.' She picked up the woven baskets she had been about to take with her on her bus trip and went with the others towards the ramshackle, dust-coated car standing in the shade of the oleander bushes.

It was wonderful out in the crystalline, early-morning air, Liz thought. Xenia, a smile on her sun-weathered brown face, was offering her a blue flower plucked from the roadside. As Liz bent her head to sniff the delicate blossom she wondered if the flower had been offered as a guard against car-sickness. A little later, as Spiro sent the car rocketing up a steep incline, she reflected that had she been a bad traveller, she would certainly be in need of the curative properties of a native herb. For the road twisted and turned and the driver travelled at alarming speed, hurtling past a man riding a donkey and taking a hairpin bend at such speed that they narrowly averted colliding with an approaching tour bus. Clutching the door handle, Liz was relieved when at length they drew up in a small settlement with its cluster of white stone cottages.

She slid out of the car, conscious of an appetising aroma of freshly baked bread that wafted from a stone bakery in the narrow, winding street. Further down the cobbled lane she noticed a small dark store with grocery lines in the window. It seemed however that her new friends were headed resolutely in the direction of the open market ahead and soon Liz was swept into the colourful confusion and noisy exuberance of the open-air stalls. Greek sailors were carrying in boxes of freshly-caught fish, red mullet and barbounia, heaping the fish on tables, and there were great woven baskets heaped with the golden Cretan oranges that Liz was certain were like no other oranges in the world. Straight away she purchased some. The next moment she realised that Xenia was frowning and shaking her head disapprovingly. Clearly, Liz thought, she had paid too high a price for the luscious fruit. So from then on she contented herself with indicating to Xenia the crisp lettuces, aubergines, huge tomatoes, peppers and onions, thereby saving herself a lot of drachmas. As a treat she purchased a portion of *kalamarakia*, pieces of young squid cooked in a tasty sauce that she had enjoyed at restaurant meals.

Much later, laden with baskets that overflowed with flour and cooking oil, fruit and vegetables, they took the road back to the villa. When they reached their destination Xenia and Nikos returned to the car to carry in a varied assortment of bags and bundles holding their personal possessions and the young Greek driver, with an impudent grin, threw a kiss to Liz before driving away.

That afternoon she lost no time before beginning her preparations for the opening of the taverna. In the kitchen she prepared rolls that later appeared fluffy and appetising from the oven. Now that they had lost the services of the Greek interpreter she imagined there might be some difficulty in explaining to Xenia the tasks she wanted done. It transpired, however, that the Greek woman, although obviously puzzled by the departure from her own traditional dishes, appeared to understand what Liz was trying to get through to her. Before long Xenia was busily slicing hard-boiled eggs and peppers and tomatoes into separate containers.

Outside, seated at one of the tables he had set out in the shade of the canopy, Nikos was fingering his worry beads and occasionally playing his lyre, his rich baritone voice raised in accompaniment to his lively native melodies.

By the end of the day the glass compartments in the cabinet were filled with fresh attractively prepared foods, and crisp freshly baked rolls were cooling on wire racks. Tomorrow, Liz mused, she would put out a notice on the taverna, OPEN, and beside it, FRESH TOASTED ROLLS. With any luck the odd hotel guest would wander in and pass on the word about the café catering for overseas tourists. Just as soon as her venture was firmly established she would let Adam in on her good fortune—and that, she promised herself, would be a moment worth waiting for! Adam . . . for a moment she stood motionless, dreaming. His kiss, his lips so clean-cut and firm, yet they could curve with humour or tenderness. Strength and tenderness, that was Adam. Aghast, she realised the direction in which her thoughts were moving and amended hurriedly, 'At least, that's what he *seems* like to anyone who doesn't really know him!'

My goodness, she marvelled the following morning, but news travels fast around here! For already guests from the nearby hotel were strolling over the hill and moving through the screen of pink oleander blossoms on their way to the bay below. Soon groups of holiday-clad people were heading for the small room at the end of the taverna that Liz had labelled Changing Room or dropping down on chairs beneath the sun-umbrellas that Nikos had set out on the sand. Before long the new arrivals were swimming and disporting themselves in the sun-sparkled waters of the bay—and everyone knew, Liz told herself gleefully, how fresh air and salt water sharpened the appetite! All at once she realised that groups of laughing, chatting people were approaching the open counter of the taverna and presently she found herself frantically coping with a rush of customers, while all around echoed a variety of accents, Canadian, American, English, even the Australian 'twang'.

As the busy day wore on Liz had time for no more than a quick smile of welcome for her customers as frenziedly she flipped rolls on the rack for toasting and mixed Nescafé in pottery mugs. Indeed, it seemed to her that no sooner had a party carried their trays to one of the tables spilling out on the sand than a fresh group took their place at the crowded counter.

Flushed with the temperature of the room and the heat of the day, Liz's shirt clung damply to her back and pespiration beaded her forehead as she worked on. All at once she became aware of a friendly feminine voice. 'We were so happy,' a charming Canadian woman was saying, 'when our bus courier told us he was taking us to a truly superb swimming beach and a taverna where we could get homecooking. My, but these rolls are just delicious!'

Liz flashed her a smile. 'I'm glad you like them!' Her

spirits were soaring. Hadn't Adam told her that in the days when her uncle lived here, tour buses had made regular stops at the taverna that was the only refreshment centre for many miles along the lonely coast? But how she wondered could word have got around so swiftly of the re-opening of the taverna on the beach? The next moment she forgot the query in a rush of filling the emptied food compartments in the cabinet.

The following days flew by for Liz in a frenzied effort to keep up with the work. She had little time to think of anything else but the tasks in hand, with time only for a brief dip in the sea after the last customer had left and the doors had been finally closed for the night.

Awakening earlier than usual the next morning, she reflected that this was only the start of the summer and if customers continued to patronise the taverna at this rate she would be able to repay the loan Kostas had given her with no trouble at all. Wonderful to think that Adam wouldn't get his way with the property deal, not this time! It was, of course, the patronage of the tour buses that made all the difference to her takings. Something niggled at the back of her mind. How had it happened that the bus driver had known the exact date on which to resume his stop for refreshments? There seemed no answer to the mystery. Put it down to local gossip, or just plain coincidence. One thing, her thoughts ran on, she must recompense Xenia and Nikos for their help at the taverna. Xenia was a wonderful asset, she couldn't manage without her assistance and Nikos—well, what if he did spend a lot of his time clicking his worry beads and chatting with his friends from the next bay as they sat at a table drinking endless tiny cups of Greek coffee? The fish he brought back after some hours spent in a caique with friends fishing in the bay were a welcome addition to the larder. And the liveliness and verve of his native songs that he sang in the evenings, to the accompaniment of his lyre, were enjoyed as much by herself as by customers. Besides, there was something about his joy of living and unfailing

Greek gallantry that she found hard to resist. The problem was, she mused, that not knowing the Greek language she hadn't a clue as to the amount of wages she should pay the couple. Katina, of course, could help her there—but nothing, she vowed, would induce her to ask help of the other girl.

Adam could advise you about all that, the sneaky thought came unbidden. He could tell you all you want to know. He was furious with her, there was no doubt of that, but all the same he could scarcely refuse to answer a simple question in the matter of wages for the Greek couple. Besides, hadn't she promised herself a visit to Adam to let him know of her fantastic change of fortune? The prospect of scoring a victory over him was intoxicating and she intended to exploit her opportunity to the full. Tonight she would no longer be just a girl from down under without family or friends or influence determined to go it alone. A girl whose dreams had faded, leaving her a temporary citizen on her own property, in danger of being forced to surrender her inheritance to the most untrustworthy, arrogant, devastatingly attractive man she had ever met! A wealthy, self-centred landowner who could, she wouldn't wonder, afford to buy up any other property he wanted. Just as he could probably have any woman he wanted—except her!

She wouldn't take up much of his time, her thoughts ran on, just a brief visit. He wouldn't get the idea, would he, that she had come to say she was sorry for the hot accusing words she had flung at him? It wasn't as if she would be humbling herself, giving him a mistaken impression that she wanted to get back to the carefree companionship of their day together at Knossos. Just a brief business call, she reasoned with herself—that wouldn't hurt, would it?

'Business my foot!' the voice deep in her mind challenged her. 'You know you long for him every day and night. Any old excuse will serve so long as you can be with him again, even if only for a few minutes!'

Rubbish! she argued with herself. She had to find an

answer to her wages problem, didn't she? And there was no reason why she shouldn't go tonight. Any tourists who came strolling down the winding goat track between the olive trees in the blue Cretan twilight would be amply catered for by Xenia, she knew. So why not?

The decision lent impetus to her tasks throughout the long tiring day. At last as the dinner hour of the tourist hotel approached the crowd at the taverna began to drift away and Liz pushed back the damp tendrils of hair from her flushed forehead and cleared away plates and coffee mugs and glasses. Later, when she had finished her chores, she approached the Greek woman, and pointed up the darkening slope. 'Hotel,' she said. 'Adam.'

Xenia's sun-wrinkled nut brown face broke into an understanding smile. Vigorously she nodded her coifed head in a reassuring gesture. *'Kali nikta!'*

'Goodnight!' Liz smiled in farewell. She knew she need have no qualms about leaving Xenia in charge of the taverna for a short while.

That evening she took her time over preparations for her visit, taking a leisurely shower and letting the water play over her sand-dusted hair. Afterwards she sprinkled fragrant talc liberally over her body. Then, clad in bra and panties, she rifled through her scanty wardrobe. Whatever happened, she mustn't look all dressed up tonight. She'd die, she'd just die, if Adam got the impression that she had prettied herself up especially for his approval, if he took the view that despite their stormy parting she was— well, interested in him.

'Aren't you?' jeered the small voice deep in her mind.

She thrust it aside and endeavoured to concentrate on what she would wear tonight. In the end she settled for a simple navy-blue T-shirt and white slacks. There, she told herself when she was dressed, that shouldn't give him any mistaken notions about the reason I've come to see him. Especially if I leave my face free of make-up and tie my hair back from my face with a ribbon for coolness.

Idly, as she slipped her feet into white thonged sandals,

she mused that as a rule when a girl got herself ready for an important date she took endless pains to look her best—for him. But not this girl! All she wanted of the meeting was to have her moment of triumph, see the shock and disbelief in Adam's eyes when she let him in on her incredible news.

And yet—she paused at the mirror for a final glance—it was odd that tonight for all her lack of feminine enhancements she looked different from usual, her face lit with an inner excitement, lips soft and tremulous, cheeks faintly flushed—*Like a girl in love.* The thought came from nowhere. What was she thinking? she derided herself, and moved to the bureau to pick up the golden pendant that Adam had given her. The bee with a sting, she reflected wryly. The tiny stylised bee held for her a facination she couldn't explain. Tonight the jewelled eyes at the end of their fine gold wires seemed to wink at her under the light. Why not? they seemed to beam a message. What harm could it do?

Still she hesitated. The fine gold chain with its glowing ornament would complement perfectly the dark navy blue top she was wearing, but because she was wearing his gift would he think—? What did she care what Adam thought? Swiftly she drew the chain around her throat, pushing aside the long fall of dark hair in order to fasten the clasp. She comforted herself with the thought that if Adam should have any ideas that sentiment for him had impelled her to wear his gift, the news she had to tell him tonight would soon disillusion him on that score. She closed the door behind her and went out into the star-ridden night.

Outside in the shadowed courtyard cicadas piped their summer song, taking her back to her own country. But on the other side of the world the cicadas would long have gone, chased away by the chill of winter. This was Crete, land of savage splendour and ancient pagan gods. Where high in the velvety night sky alien stars blazed in place of the familiar golden kite of the Southern Cross hanging over the Pacific ocean. And all that mattered to her was Adam. She scarcely realised she was hurrying until her sandals felt rough to her bare feet and she paused on the goat track to shake away any sandy soil. Why was she hurrying? she asked herself. Only because she couldn't *wait* to see Adam's face when she told him her news.

All at once she was struck by a dismaying thought. Suppose he should chance to be away from home tonight? She thrust the unwelcome possibility aside. She had been so lucky, surely nothing could go wrong now! Even if he has heard rumours of the taverna being open again I still want to see him, to tell him about it myself, she thought.

As she came over the top of the rise she could see the windows of the high building below ablaze with light and soon she was hurrying across the wide concrete surround of the hotel and into the foyer, hoping all the time that tonight Katina would not be on duty there. Once again, however, luck was with her, because a Greek girl who was seated at the reception desk, answered Liz's enquiry with a smile.

'Yes, he is in, I know,' she said in perfect English. 'Come with me and wait in the lounge while I tell him you are here.' Liz went with the Greek girl into the vast lounge room with its deep luxurious seating and great floor-to-ceiling windows looking out on a dark turbulent sea. As she went on, heads turned to watch the progress of the girl whose wide excited eyes and softly parted lips radiated an air of youth and vitality.

Liz realised that groups of guests were scattered around the immense room. Dark-eyed, elegantly gowned Greek women and foreign tourists enjoying a brief stay at the luxurious hotel on their tour of the Greek islands, expensively gowned women and men wearing light-coloured linen suits.

Liz, seating herself in one of the deep upholstered chairs in a corner of the room, tried not to show her awareness of the admiring glances beamed in her direction by middle-aged men standing at the bar and a young Greek waiter who was carrying drinks on a tray. Even a group of Greek businessmen seated at a nearby table had paused in the clicking of their worry beads to eye her appreciatively. For heaven's sake, was she the only young girl in the entire room? A swift glance around her told her that she was right in her assumption. But of course, she mused, the tour buses taking guests on sightseeing expeditions over the island would be patronised by older folk with time on their hands. This lavishly appointed hotel with its marble entrance hall and spacious grounds would be way beyond the price range of young people with packs on their backs making their own way through the Greek islands.

The next moment she forgot everything else in the room, for Adam was striding towards her, an impressive masculine figure. Tonight, seeing him wearing a formal suit, it struck her that he looked every inch the owner of his luxurious domain. Authoritative, assured, a man who was accustomed to giving orders—except where she was concerned, of course!

'Liz!' At the warmth in his voice her heart gave a great leap, then settled again. The way he was smiling towards her, the deep soft look in his eyes, anyone would think that he was more than delighted to see her. Anyone who didn't really know him, that was, she reminded herself the next moment.

He dropped down in a chair facing her. 'Great to see you!' The expression in his eyes underlined the commonplace words.

Just in time the thought came to her that there might be good reason for the warmth of his welcome. Could it be that he was expecting her to say 'Sorry, Adam' for the accusing words she had flung at him at their last meeting? Or more likely he was of the opinion she had come here to let him know that the property deal could go through after all.

'I didn't expect to see *you* tonight.' He spoke lightly, but his eyes met hers gravely.

'Liz shifted uneasily, for the unspoken words 'after the

way we parted' hung between them. She ignored the unspoken implication of his remark and rushed into speech. 'I thought you'd be surprised!' She smiled up at him and thought how easy it was to smile tonight. The difficult thing was to keep the triumph from showing in her eyes. 'I had to see you,' she grinned, 'on business! Would you believe?'

Instantly he was alert, the grey eyes that seemed to see so much more than she wanted them to fixed on her face.

'I just wanted to tell you,' the dancing light in her eyes intensified and she couldn't keep the note of elation from her voice, 'that I won't be needing those worry beads you bought me in Knossos after all!'

'No?' His voice was careless as though he were scarcely interested in her affairs, but there was a deep attentive look in his eyes. 'Come into a fortune, from another uncle, is that it?'

She laughed merrily. 'As good as! You'd never believe what's happened!'

'Try me.' At the softness and warmth of his glance, almost she could believe he was really interested in her news, regardless of how it might affect his own interests.

'You know all those electrical goods I needed for starting up the taverna again? Well,' she announced breathlessly, 'I've got them all now—the lot!'

She nodded excitedly. 'I've got the OPEN sign on the taverna already! It was after our trip to Knossos—' hastily she glossed over the day of such happiness that it now seemed unreal, a day that had ended on such a bitter note. 'I was down on the beach all day and when I got back just before dark there were tyre marks all around the taverna, and when I went inside—wait for it—there was a deep-freeze and a frozen food cabinet and the toasting machine I needed, all installed and ready to go. And exactly,' she cried in triumph, 'the measurements I'd written out. So of course I knew who'd sent it all.'

At his interrogative lift of dark brows she said promptly,

'Kostas, of course. He must have had the whole load sent out from the store at Heraklion. It's as clear as can be. There's just no one else it could be! Know something, Adam?' Without waiting for his comments she ran on. 'He must have had second thoughts about letting me have his personal loan to buy the things I needed to start up in business. I guess,' she added slowly, 'I have you to thank for it all really.'

'How so?'

She said thoughtfully, 'I've been thinking over all you told me about Greek men not thinking kindly about a countryman of theirs who takes advantage of a woman on her own. Kostas must have been furious at being caught out doing just that. And then for you to knock him down must have hurt his dignity more than his chin! I bet when he got back to his office he got to thinking things over and decided the best way out of the situation was to let me have the loan I wanted. A lot better for him than your letting on to his business friends in Heraklion—' She broke off. 'You haven't, have you?'

He shook his head. 'Not me.'

'Well, he won't know that. For all he knows he might be losing a lot of his clients. I figured it out that the only way he could try to make things right would be to get on the phone, put the order for me through, and have the stuff delivered. I looked all over the place for a receipt with his name on it, but I couldn't find even a delivery slip. Not that I'm worrying about that, he must have paid for it all or the firm wouldn't have delivered it to me. I expect he'll post me the papers to sign before long. I shouldn't imagine,' she flashed a smile, 'that he'll be calling on me at the villa this time! Aren't I lucky!'

'Congratulations!' There was an enigmatic note in his tone.

'That's just the start of the good news,' she ran on. 'You should have seen the crowd that came over the hill to swim in the bay and order refreshments of filled toasted rolls at the taverna! There were ever so many, I think they came from your hotel here. And then, later in the afternoon, 'her blue-grey eyes glowed with excitement,' a tour bus arrived and it seems that's going to be on a regular basis, three times a week!' She clapped her hands together. 'It's fantastic! And if that wasn't enough for one day, who do you think turned up on my doorstep? Nikos and Xenia!' Her laughter rang out. 'Nikos looked like a brigand—that ferocious-looking moustache of his and knee-boots and the beaded black veil thing on his forehead that all the older Crete men seem to wear. We finally got things sorted out with the help of a young Greek boy who'd driven them to the villa in his car. I remembered your telling me about the couple who used to help my uncle and—' she hesitated over the name, 'Katina, in the taverna. Nikos and Xenia must have kept an ear to the ground to know just the time when they might be needed again. Now we're getting along fine. Xenia's catching on fast about preparing different sorts of food from what she's used to and Nikos has promised to catch lots of fish for the table. Me, I'm learning a lot about how to hand customers their change in drachmas.'

'Good for you!' Once again she surprised an unreadable look in his eyes. 'So you're in business?'

She nodded happily. 'As from now! Things have just fallen into my lap! I really can't believe my good luck! Those Greek gods must really be on my side!'

'Looks like it.' His tone was flat, almost uninterested. Indeed, Liz mused, if she hadn't known how absurd was the thought, she could imagine that his interest was centred on her rapt young face rather than in what she was telling him. Unable to sustain his brilliant gaze any longer, she dropped her eyes and tried to pick up the threads of her story.

'This calls for a drink,' he was saying, and beckoned to a young Greek waiter on the other side of the room. 'What would you like?'

'Not retsina.' Liz wrinkled her nose at him. 'I just can't get used to the pine flavour. Oh, I know there's a Cretan saying that it takes six glasses before you know if you like it, but one was enough for me!'

Adam grinned. 'There's a native wine they make from rosaki grapes grown around here. I think you'll like it.'

'I'll try it. Well, that's the good news!' A flush of excitement burned high on her delicate cheekbones and she drew a deep breath. Now for that long-awaited moment of triumph! 'And now for the bad!' She ran on in a rush of words, 'I won't be selling out to you after all!'

'No?' He appeared entirely unperturbed, she thought bewilderedly. His air of polite indifference was maddening, sparking her to defiance. The impulsive words fell from her lips before she could stop them. 'You don't seem very disappointed about all this?'

His lean dark face was impassive. 'Should I be?' he enquired blandly.

Liz looked at him suspiciously. He was being deliberately obtuse, of course. Oh, she might have known he would give nothing away. Conscious of a sense of letdown, she eyed him uncertainly. The speeches she had carefully rehearsed fled from her mind and she murmured, 'But what about you?' The way in which he was leaning back in his chair, regarding her with cool detachment, was making her thoughts churn in confusion.

'I'll get by.' At the cool amusement in his tone she realised how utterly naïve she had been ever to have imagined that Adam would give her the satisfaction of betraying the slightest sign of emotion at her news. Stupid, stupid of her not to have realised that this arrogant, oh-so-attractive male would never admit to her having scored a victory over him.

With a sense of relief she turned to find the waiter setting down wine glasses on a low table between them. When the young Greek had left them, Adam raised his glass. 'Let's drink to the success of your taverna, shall we?'

She gathered herself together and managed a bright smile. 'In the Cretan way?'

'What else?'

The crystal goblets rang like a bell as they curved their hands around glasses in the traditional gesture and clinked them together, at the same time murmuring the customary 'Hyrr, Hyrr', rolling the 'Rs' in sibilant accents echoing the vibrations of wine-filled goblets. It was a sound that had the effect of sending them both into laughter.

Could it be the sweet and relaxing wine, Liz found herself wondering a little later, or was it the heady sensation of finding herself free to put her plans into action, that was going to her head, making her say to Adam, 'I just can't believe it! You don't seem to be one little bit sorry about my staying on in Crete.'

His eyes, compelling and enigmatic, held hers. 'Why should I be disappointed about that?'

All at once she was flustered. 'I—I—' She tried to gather her thoughts together. 'That wasn't the only reason I came to see you tonight.'

'No?' Deep in his eyes tiny flames flickered and something in his gaze made her forget all about Nikos and Xenia and the matter of their wages. Dropping her eyes, she studied the white wine in her glass. 'It's funny,' the words seemed to fall from her lips without her volition, 'but I got the idea you were anxious to have those properties in the bay.'

'That's right.' His tone was laconic. 'I still am, actually.'

'But you don't seem to mind a scrap about my not selling out?'

He set down his wine glass. 'Why should I worry?' There was a mocking intonation in his tone. 'Sooner or later I'll have it. Just a matter of waiting.'

'W-waiting?' She stared at him, nonplussed. 'What on earth for?'

His glance held hers until she felt she was drowning in those brilliant depths. 'For you to say "yes", of course.'

She looked at him in bewilderment. 'You'll be wasting

your time, then! You'll never persuade me to let them go, so you might just as well give up and call it a day right now.'

'Oh, I wouldn't say that,' he returned with deceptive mildness, 'I've got a lot of faith in my success with plan number two.' His bright gaze challenged her. 'I'll be getting it off the ground any minute now.'

Startled, she regarded him in amazement. 'You're having me on! But if this brilliant project of yours has anything to do with me—'

'Sure has!' His mocking grin sparked her to say with spirit, 'Then you haven't a hope!'

'Want to bet?' He studied her flushed face. 'I'll tell you something, young Liz, I usually get what I want.'

'Not this time,' flared Liz. Some devil inside her made her add, 'If it's anything like that last plan of yours—' She must have imagined the look of hurt in his eyes, she told herself. He couldn't *really* care about the barb she had hurled at him, not Adam. The silence seemed to last for ever and she thought with an odd pang of regret, why did I say that? But he deserved it, didn't he? She regarded him from under her eyelashes and said lightly, 'Anyway, what is this big project of yours?'

Unexpectedly he grinned. She *must* have imagined that fleeting glimpse of pain in his eyes. 'Perfectly simple, really, but it's got great potential—if I can pull it off.'

Liz said, pouting, 'You might explain it to me, seeing it's such a master plan. Or don't you think,' she enquired laughingly, 'that I know enough about Greek hotel management to understand what you're aiming for?'

There was a veiled expression in his eyes. 'Oh, you'll understand this one all right.'

'Well, then—?'

'Later, later,' he waved the matter away with a lift of a sun-bronzed hand. 'Don't rush me!'

His soft laugh was infuriating. 'Let's just wait and see. Meantime,' he got to his feet and the touch of his hand on her bare arm sent a tremor running through her, 'let's dance, shall we?'

Liz was only too glad to put an end to the conversation. For she sensed in Adam a power and determination that undermined all her defences. And what if she should betray to him how vulnerable she was?

As they moved together to the rhythm of a popular dance number Liz's thoughts were in a tumult. Oh, it was heavenly to be with Adam tonight with no complications to come between them. From now on, she thought with elation, whenever he looks at me with the special glance he seems to keep just for me, it *will* be for myself. The unfamiliar feeling was intoxicating, and all at once nothing else in the world mattered but just being here, with him.

It was several dances later when she turned to him with a smile. 'I only meant to stop for a few minutes. I'd better be getting along. I'm a working girl now, remember?'

'If you wish.' A little to her disappointment Adam made no attempt to detain her. But he would see her back along the winding track through the olive trees, she consoled herself. Her senses were whirling and an irrational happiness surged through her. When he kisses me goodnight in the courtyard I'll let him know, in the subtle ways that every woman knows, that from now on everything will be different between us, she thought. No more conflicts over property, that would be all in the past, for who could give serious thought to that ridiculous idea of Adam's that he called his 'plan number two'? No more subterfuges, she promised herself. Adam, his arms closing around her in the shadows of the deserted courtyard. Her senses quickened at the thought.

They were moving over the expanse of carpeted floor and had reached the foyer when an imperious feminine voice halted them. 'Adam!'

Liz's gaze went to the marble staircase where a woman leaned over the balustrade, looking down on them. Liz had a swift impression of a tall woman, slim as a wand, a dark-haired beauty wearing a low-cut black dress shot with rippling silver.

'Don't be long, will you?' It was Liz thought with a stab of the heart, a possessive, *intimate*-sounding voice. 'Don't forget the tiz that Bill and Lena got into the last time we kept them waiting.'

Adam glanced up towards the glittering figure above, then gave a brief nod. 'It's okay.' He turned to lay a hand on Liz's arm, guiding her out through the imposing entrance and out into the soft darkness of the night.

Liz felt cold shivers creep through her body. All at once it came to her with painful clarity what a fool she had been to burst in on Adam as she had done, without warning. To have imagined in her blind trusting way that merely because tonight he had seemed warm and friendly, ignoring the circumstances of their previous stormy parting, that he really wanted to be with her, that he was even glad that she was staying on Crete, no matter the effect on his property plans. Oh, she might have known, she mused bitterly, the formal suit he was wearing, his familiar attitude towards the exquisitely dressed sophisticated-looking woman who radiated an air of self-confidence—and something else, a close relationship with Adam. She must have been crazy—the bleak thoughts rushed through her mind—to have imagined he cared for her a lot, even when there was no likelihood of her selling him her stake in this Greek island. Damn, damn, damn! she thought, hating herself for her impulsive gesture in coming here to see him tonight.

As they reached the edge of the lighted area she wrenched herself around to face him. 'Don't trouble to see me back to the villa!' Even to her own ears her laugh held a forced note. 'It's not as if I don't know the way!'

'No trouble.' He linked his hand in hers, and vibrations ran along her nerves. Determinedly she fought off the weakness. She was vulnerable to his touch, it was something that was beyond her control, and she had a sneaking suspicion that he was well aware of the effect he had on her.

The crashing disappointment she had suffered hardened her resolve and she snatched her hand from his grip. ''Night!' She was off, running up the narrow dusty track, not daring to glance back over her shoulder for fear he was following her. The next minute the query was answered for her as she tripped over a loose stone and fell to the ground, crushing the wildflowers in her headlong fall. Even before she had time to get to her feet, he had caught her up in his arms. He held her at arm's length, his tone anxious. 'You're all right, Liz?'

'Of course I am,' she mumbled, and put up a hand to wipe away the dust from her cheek.

'Sure?' His tone was warm and solicitous. But pity, she told herself, was something she couldn't take, not from him. 'You don't need to waste your time!' she flared, and struggled to free herself. He merely held her closer to him and once again she fought the excitement of his nearness, the delicious lassitude that threatened to take over. Think of his girl-friend, she told herself wildly, the scintillating figure in black and silver, the one he can't wait to get back to. It worked, giving her sufficient strength of mind to drag herself back to sanity. 'I don't need you!' she flung at him.

'Stop arguing, Liz, I'm coming with you!' There was no breaking the pressure of his fingers on her own. When they reached the courtyard he still held her hand in his. 'There's not much wrong with you, Liz, not when you bound along that goat track like a mountain goat. What was all the rush to get here?'

She said stiffly, 'I know you're in a hurry to get back tonight—'

'Me?' For a moment he sounded puzzled. Then, 'Oh, Karen, you mean?' His tone was careless. 'She'll keep.'

He was impossible! she thought angrily. Clearly a man who was so attractive to women he could have any one he wanted. He had the nerve to keep a glamorous-looking girl waiting, and to think nothing of it. He used women for his own advantage, it seemed in the same way that he had used her.

When they reached the shadows of the courtyard she wrenched her fingers from his grasp. 'Thanks for seeing me home,' she muttered and slipped away.

'Liz!' The disarming softness of his tone caught her unawares and she turned to face him. 'Haven't you forgotten something?' and before she could make an answer, 'This.' The next moment his lips sought hers in a kiss that sent fire running through her veins. Over the tumult of emotion surging through her she willed herself to passivity, while all the time her traitorous body urged her to respond to his ardent caress. At last she pulled herself free. 'I've got to go,' she murmured in a low voice, and sped towards the dark doorway.

'Wait! Come back! There's something—'

But now she was determined not to allow herself to surrender to Adam's beguiling tone or to the emotions he so easily aroused in her. Her hands were shaking, so she had difficulty in fitting the key into the lock, but at last she let herself in to the darkened house and slammed the heavy door shut behind her. Not that she need have troubled herself over him making an attempt to follow her, she realised the next minute. By now he would be taking the twisting track over the hill.

Tears trickled down her dust-smeared cheeks and she brushed them away with the back of her hand. To Adam she was no more than a stubborn girl who stood in the way of his money-making schemes, someone who had held him up tonight and caused him to be late for his dinner date with the glamorous-looking woman who had hailed him from the stairway of the hotel. Her heavy thoughts ran on. As a put-down to Adam her meeting with him tonight had been a miserable failure. He hadn't cared, he just hadn't cared about her or the property sale—not any more. All he was interested in was the eye-catching woman who spoke to him with a *belonging* note in her voice.

Liz turned away, sick at heart. She might have known that Adam would have women as friends, companions—lovers? He was a type of man to whom women would be attracted—look who's talking, she told herself bitterly. The lean dark intelligent face and male magnetism that you could almost *feel* when you were with him was a combination hard to resist, didn't she know it? So why did she feel this sickness in her midriff as if she had suffered a dreadful blow? Slowly she went into her room. Funny, she now had what she had so desperately desired, a chance to stay on in Crete to make her own way and be financially independent. Somehow, though, the matter no longer seemed of great importance. Only Adam mattered, and she knew now that he wasn't worth the anguish and heartache she had let herself in for. Somehow, she told herself on a sob, she would just have to forget him—if she could!

CHAPTER NINE

Now Liz was thankful for the long hours she had to spend working in the taverna. In the rare periods when no customers waited at the counter to be attended to, there was always cleaning to be seen to. And the baking of rolls . . . and more rolls. When the last customer had gone Liz ran down to the dark sea for a quick dip, then, too exhausted for anything else, she fell into bed. One thing, she told herself bleakly, the hard daily grind kept her from dwelling endlessly on thoughts of Adam—or did it actually work out that way? Not really, for when she was asleep she couldn't help herself, dreaming that Adam was with her once again, standing looking down at her from his lean height, his gaze warm with tenderness and *real* feeling for her.

At odd moments during the day she gave a passing thought to the letter she was expecting daily from Kostas, but so far she had received no notification from him regarding his loan. Maybe next month?

One day she was horrified to realise that she had been so absorbed in hard physical toil and her own emotional problems, she hadn't yet kept her promise to her friend and neighbour at home, to deliver the gifts and messages from Angeliké to the family in their mountain village. Swiftly she scribbled a note to Angeliké's mother, telling her she would be coming to visit her very soon and then she slipped the letter in the post. Maybe, she thought, Xenia would tell her how to get to the village. When later in the day she enquired of the Greek woman, Xenia broke into a spate of Greek, all the time gesticulating wildly. Liz was lucky, though, because a customer, a middle-aged man who happened to be standing at the counter, had taken in Liz's perplexed expression.

'Could I be of help? I happen to know the language.'

Liz turned towards him thankfully. 'Oh, please!'

'Your friend is trying to tell you that the bus for the village you mentioned leaves from the hotel stop around the point every Tuesday around two o'clock.'

'Tuesday? That's tomorrow—super!' As Liz poured coffee for her customer her thoughts were busy.'I wonder,' she smiled across at the English tourist standing at the counter, 'would you mind explaining to Xenia, she's my helper, that I'll be going to the village tomorrow and leaving her in charge here?'

He smiled in assent. Indeed, Liz thought a few moments later, there were smiles all around.

In the morning she stowed in her travel pack the gifts that Angeliké had entrusted to her for the Cretan family. She arrived very early at the bus stop and chances were she mused, that she would have a long wait. She might even have an accidental meeting with Adam. The thought came without her volition and she thrust it away. As it happened, however, while waiting in the shade of the hotel balcony, she saw neither Adam nor Katina but only a crowd of tourists who alighted from a coach.

The local bus when it pulled up beside her was crowded with peasants, the women laden with an assortment of bundles. Liz pushed her way past bearded Greek Orthodox priests in their dark robes and tall black hats and found a seat at the side of a coifed swarthy-faced woman whose bright smile revealed blackened teeth. In the noisy exuberance of the passengers, speech was impossible even had she known the language, so she nodded and smiled to a peasant woman seated opposite her who was holding towards her a flower plucked from a bunch of red and white lilies that had no doubt been gathered from her own garden this morning. Liz was becoming accustomed to this national characteristic of the Greek peasants to enjoy giving pleasure to strangers. Nor did their goodness of heart extend only to strangers, she reflected, eyeing the peasant women with their labelled bundles, each of which was no doubt a gift for a friend or neighbour. A bunch of grapes maybe, or a pot of home-made jam or a jar of olives.

As they moved up the sun-dried slopes Liz was only vaguely aware of the scarlet poppies and golden daisies that flourished alongside the roadside or the sails of turning windmills, white against the blue of distant hills. As always when she had time to dream her mind wandered to Adam. Once she had thought of him in the same way as the early Cretans had regarded their pagan god Zeus, someone to be looked up to, to trust, to love. *Don't think of him.*

They had been travelling for a long time under a scorching sun when she realised they were approaching a small village. Presently, together with the rest of the voluble, chattering passengers, Liz got out of the vehicle and moved into the dim interior of an ornately decorated church with its time-worn altar, richly coloured ikons and flickering candles. Something of the silence and peacefulness of the age-old place of worship eased a little her sense of heartache.

It was later, when they had left the main highway and turned into a rough metal road, that Liz realised there was another vehicle on the lonely road. Idly watching, she saw that the red car had passed them to speed ahead, then pull up at the side of the road. For some reason, the driver was honking his horn, evidently as a signal for the bus to stop. Liz couldn't see any more, for as the bus ground to a halt, excited passengers left their seats and crowded around the driver talking and gesticulating wildly. Lost in her own heavy thoughts, Liz wasn't terribly interested in what was happening, then all at once her heart gave a great leap, then settled again. Adam! She would know his deep vibrant tones anywhere! All at once she became aware that all heads were turned in her direction and everyone was talking at once. Swiftly she got up from her seat and the excited, chattering passengers gave way to her as she made her way forward. She was conscious of Adam's tall figure, his searching glance moving in her direction, then before she knew what was happening, he had clasped her hand in a no-nonsense grip and was drawing her down the bus step and out on to the rough road.

From the vehicle she could hear shouts and laughter and loud calls in Greek. 'What on earth—?'

He was practically dragging her across the road and towards his car. 'In with you!'

But Liz refused to be manhandled in this autocratic way. She had had enough already of Adam's high-handed treatment. 'I don't know that I want to come with you,' she shook herself free of his detaining arm. 'What's all this about anyway?'

'You're coming to the village with me,' his tone was curt, 'it will be much more comfortable for you than that crowded bus.'

Still she hung back. 'I don't mind the bus. I rather like it.'

'Well, make up your mind.' His mouth was set and stern. 'Are you coming with me or not?' The staccato tone, so different from the soft accents she had known, sparked her to snap back.

'I haven't much option, have I?' For at that moment the bus lumbered past, the passengers hanging out of windows to wave and shout and call out in a flood of Greek.

'Not unless you want to walk the rest of the way,' Adam agreed. 'It's quite a step back to the villa too,' he added offhandedly.

'Oh, all right, then!' She made to hurry into the car, but he was before her, flinging open the passenger door and when she had seated herself, tucking her white pleated skirt out of the way.

They moved along the road through a cloud of dust raised by the vehicle ahead and Liz, stealing a glance towards the strong masculine profile at her side, decided that he didn't deserve being spoken to! First of all he had let her down in that sneaky underhanded way, then he had told her nothing about his girl-friend (don't forget that, her heart reminded her). Now he had abducted her from a public vehicle—well, she thought crossly, you could call it an abduction. He made her so *mad*! she fumed silently. On top of all that, she thought rebelliously, he was ignoring her, staring at the road ahead without even a polite word, let alone giving her an explanation for his extraordinary conduct. Anger mounted in her. But she would soon change all that, she vowed, and heard her own voice saying too breathlessly, too quickly, 'Dragging me off the bus in that high-handed way—' The laugh she had intended to be mocking, a trifle sarcastic, sounded even to her own ears, affected and stupid. 'Heaven only knows,' she flung at him accusingly, 'what the Greek passengers thought of it all!' She glanced up at him and her traitorous heart turned over. His strong profile looked as though it was carved in bronze. With an effort she brought her mind back to his cool tones. 'They wouldn't have missed that little episode for worlds! They were enjoying every moment of it!'

'What!' she gasped. 'But you—you—' she spluttered indignantly, 'for all they knew you might have been a complete stranger to me!' She warmed to her theme. 'The way it looked you could have been intending to hold me to ransom or—or anything! You could see they were excited about it!'

'Oh, they were excited all right! All that hullabaloo and waving to us out of the bus window.' He threw her a sardonic glance. 'All the same, they didn't look all that worried about you, would you say?'

'I guess not,' she admitted reluctantly. Now that she came to consider the matter the Greek peasants had had more the air of a wildly excited audience witnessing an exciting drama than people who were horrified at the unexpected happening and fearful of her welfare at the hands of a stranger. Curiosity got the better of her and she couldn't stop the words that had risen to her lips. 'Well then, you know the language, what did they imagine was happening?'

'They weren't too surprised. This sort of thing happens every now and again with the mountain folk of Crete. They still stick to their ancient ways. They're a bit out of touch with modern living and the primitive customs still hold good. It was a new twist to an old story, though, for them to see it all happen on a bus!' Adam's voice was deadpan, his gaze fixed on the rough metal road ahead as he swung the car around a hairpin bend.

Liz was so astonished at his words that she forgot her anger. She looked up at him with puzzled eyes. 'What on earth do you mean?'

'Oh, they just thought I was abducting you!'

'Well,' exclaimed Liz on an outraged breath, 'of all the—'

'It's quite a custom,' Adam cut in smoothly, 'when you get far enough away from the cities. You'd be surprised how many Cretan marriages start off with the bride being carried off by force by her suitor. It does settle the question, though it can cause a feud between families that can go on for generations!'

'I don't wonder!' Liz cried indignantly. The next moment, becoming aware of the twist of amusement in Adam's well-shaped lips, she hastened to change the subject. 'How far,' she asked breathlessly, 'do we have to go before we reach the village?'

He shrugged. 'Your guess is as good as mine, but I'd give it another thirty minutes. It's hard to say for sure—people living up here go along on Cretan time, say the time it takes to smoke a cigarette or for the sky to darken.'

Liz was scarcely listening, relieved out of all proportion to the cause, by his change of subject. Her cheeks burned hotly at the thought of his explanation of the Cretan peasant's view of the affair. And to think she had begged him to tell her!

A little later she voiced the question that tugged at her mind. 'What I can't understand is how you knew that I was making this trip today.'

'That's an easy one to answer. I just happened to take a phone call from your friend up in the mountains. Seems she didn't get your letter saying you were planning a visit to them until today and she was hoping to be able to stop you from making the trip today. They wanted to arrange for someone to meet you at the village and take you on to their house, but I told them it was too late as you'd already have taken off in the bus that I could see disappearing in the distance. So then I accepted their warm invitation to come along too. Friendly people, the Cretans. They wouldn't understand anyone turning down their hospitality, so what could I do?'

Liz felt her cheeks flame with the humiliating realisation that he had put himself out for her, and once again she found herself in his debt. The thought made her say crossly, 'You needn't have troubled—'

A shrug of broad shoulders. 'No trouble. I happened to have a free day and I've always promised myself a run in the car to take a look at one of those mountain villages. Up till now I've never made it.'

She looked at him suspiciously, but his expression told her nothing. If that really was the reason for his chasing after her, she didn't feel so bad about his making the long trip on her behalf. But there was something about his blandly innocent stare that said, 'You'd better believe me.' She said very low, 'So long as that was the only reason—'

His sideways glance was disconcerting. 'What else?'

Stupidly, she tried for the last word. 'I'd have been quite all right, you know. I'm used to getting around by myself.'

'In the Cretan mountains?' There was a satirical note in his voice.

All at once she felt a pang of contrition. She supposed she did owe him some gratitude for his action today. She murmured reluctantly, 'Well, thanks anyway.'

'My pleasure.' The edge to his tone gave the lie to the words. Oh well—Liz stared resentfully at the hills with their silvery green foliage of olive trees—she had tried to thank him. Why couldn't he come right out with it and tell her the truth, that being forced into spending the entire day with her was the last thing in the world he would have chosen to do, and only a sense of politeness had impelled him to make the journey?

He seemed to tune in on her thoughts. 'Interesting country up this way. Like I said, it's all new to me.'

She flung him a swift upward glance, but his gaze was fixed on the curve of road ahead. 'Who knows,' he added in a careless tone, 'you might be glad of an interpreter around when you get amongst all those relations of your neighbour at home.'

Swiftly she dismissed the offer.

'Oh, I don't think there'll be any problem about that,' she said airily. 'Angeliké told me that her brother has lived for years in America and he'll be able to pass on all the messages I've brought for the family.'

Adam's mouth tightened. 'I get it.'

There was a cool politeness, about his tone that told her he was still angry with her. Why then, she wondered confusedly, had he gone out of his way to see her to her destination today? It was just another thing about him she would never understand. Just because he insisted on accompanying her to the mountain village, she told herself hotly, that wasn't to say that they could get back to their old footing, and if he was expecting her to feel differently towards him, he would soon find out his error. To drive home her point she maintained a chilly silence.

They had been driving inland for some miles. Now there was nothing to be seen but the mountain crags, the only sound the faraway tinkle of sheep bells. Once a great golden eagle swooped from a high crag, dark against the sun. It was a remote, unreal world, Liz mused. The next moment she was wrenched from her thoughts by Adam's voice. 'Not far from here down a ravine is the cave where, according to the myths, Zeus was born. Interested in Cretan mythology?'

Liz forgot all about maintaining a dignified silence. 'Oh, I am! I am! Who could help being interested?' She gazed out at the mountainous country around them. 'In places like this it would be easy to believe in those pagan gods and goddesses and nymphs. I'll never forget the frescoes at Knossos with pictures of the priest-king and the bull-leaping—'

'And the pendant of the honey-bee,' drawled Adam, his gaze fixed on the white dusty road. 'You liked the original when you saw it in the museum at Heraklion?'

'Oh yes, *yes*!' He had taken her by surprise. 'It's an exquisite thing, and the funny part of it is that it could easily have been made by a present-day goldsmith.'

'But you don't wear the replica,' his cold voice probed. 'Why not?'

'No.'

Her thoughts raced in confusion. She could scarcely confess to this hard-eyed man that it was the giver of the pendant to whom she had come to feel differently.

He appeared, however, to have lost interest in the matter. If only she still had faith in him!

Suddenly they swept around a bend to come in sight of a church, a cluster of white stone cottages and a tree-shaded square in the centre of a village. 'This is the last stop for bus passengers', Adam told her. Liz couldn't help the thought that the journey would have been hot and tiring in the overcrowded vehicle compared with the cool comfort of Adam's red car. Not that she would give him the satisfaction of knowing her thoughts in the matter.

He was guiding the car down the main street, and presently he drew up in the shade of a leafy tree where a Cretan youth stood waiting with two donkeys.

All at once Liz realised the significance of the mounts. She swung around to face Adam. 'You've arranged for donkeys to take us the rest of the way? Golly!' She burst into laughter. 'Now I know why the Greek driver on the bus got so worked up about my walking the distance, whatever it is. I suppose it's way up some mountain track?'

'So I gather.' Unfolding his long length from the driving seat, he went around the car to open the passenger door.

'This is fun!' Liz stepped out on to the dusty road. For a moment she forgot her companion, her attention centred on the strong mountain animals with their wooden saddles that were thickly padded with scarlet blankets.

She waited while Adam spoke in the Greek language with the swarthy youth, who was waving his arms and gesticulating wildly. A short time ago she would have suspected some dreadful danger lay on the route ahead, but she was becoming accustomed to the Cretan's excitable speech and lightning changes of mood.

'Up you go!' said Adam. Their glances met and something leaped in his eyes. The next minute he was hoisting her up into the cumbrous slatted saddle, holding her closer than he need, so that through the confusion of her senses she felt the warmth of his chest through his cotton shirt. How could she make herself hate him when she was a prisoner to the leaping of her senses every time he touched her?

'Thanks,' she whispered, and averted her gaze, fearful of what he might read there.

Presently the Cretan youth whose name was Giorgios, was leading the strong animals. Like all Greeks he was loquacious and volatile, and Liz watching his rapid gestures and flashing eyes, and listening to his spate of Greek, could only guess at that conversation between the agile dark-haired youth and Adam.

Presently they were taking a track winding down a rocky gorge leading to a river bed below. It was a scene, Liz thought, of wild splendour where pewter clouds heavy with moisture hung over the crags high above them, a silent world broken only by the clip-clop of donkeys' hooves on the rocky surface. And she was here in this magic spot, *with Adam*! Somehow today she was finding it very hard to hate Adam. Their mounts were walking abreast and it seemed silly and childish to hide herself away in a resentful silence. Especially, she mused wryly, when there were so many questions she wanted to put to him about their journey. So long as she didn't lose sight of his real reason for cultivating her acquaintance she told herself, and didn't forget about the woman he *really* loved . . .

The party followed the river bed for a long time, the donkeys picking their way amongst boulders as they followed the gorge leading ever deeper into the mountains. Never, she thought, had she been in so lonely a place, the only sign of civilization a shepherd's hut. It was as they paused for a short rest that she caught the far-away tinkle of bells. 'Would they be sheep?' she enquired of Adam.

'The *kria kia*,' he told her, 'the mountain goats. There'll be a herd of them somewhere on a patch of grassland out of sight. They don't have so much of the good life these days, not like in pagan times when they were worshipped as gods.' All at once there drifted towards them the thin, haunting notes of a shepherd's flute. 'The sheep will be somewhere down in the valleys.'

As they moved on Liz glanced up at the forbidding crags above. 'I suppose we will get to the village some time today?'

He grinned. 'Giorgios tells me we're almost there. One more climb and we'll be in the village street.' His voice softened. 'How are you feeling? Tired?'

'Oh *no!*' Her voice was alive with enthusiasm. 'I'm loving every single minute of it!' It's odd, she thought the next minute, but it's the truth. Who wouldn't enjoy the ride, she told herself, in these exciting, unfamiliar surroundings, with Adam? She thrust aside the disturbing question and tried to concentrate on clinging to her mount as he picked his way around the rocks on a steep rise. Then they reached the summit to find themselves in a small village that was ringed with mountains.

'Looks like the welcome committee's bang on time,' observed Adam, for hurrying towards them was a swashbuckling-looking Cretan of middle age with a fierce moustache. He wore dark blue baggy trousers and jackboots and an embroidered blue waistcoat, and as he came leaping down the cobbled lane, his arms waving wildly in gestures of welcome, it seemed to Liz that even his heavy black moustache was quivering with excitement. It's Petros, she thought as he came nearer. She recognised

Angeliké's father from the photographs his daughter had shown her on the other side of the world in far away New Zealand.

'*Kalimera!*'

From her seat on the donkey, Liz greeted the stranger with a smile. 'Elizabeth, Angeliké, New Zealand.' She turned towards Adam. 'Adam . . . friend.'

Petros's dark eyes flashed and Liz listened bewilderedly as a flood of Greek words poured around her. Raising her hands in a gesture of helplessness, she sent a mute appeal to Adam.

He responded with a grin. 'He's trying to tell you that you're more than welcome and that his home is at the end of the village. He'll show you the way, he says.'

'That's super!'

The donkeys' hooves made a clip-clop sound on the cobbles as the little party made their way down the narrow street. The only sign of life appeared to be a taverna where a group of swarthy Cretans glanced up from their seats at tables in the smoke-filled room, to watch with interest the calvacade that was passing.

Petros paused at last at an entrance to a white stone cottage and leaving Giogios to attend to the donkeys, Petros led them inside. Liz gained a swift impression of white walls hung with ikons and flickering oil lamps, a loom beside an open fireplace. The next moment a black-robed woman came through an archway in the room to greet her. 'Elizabet—' In the ensuing spate of Greek Liz could distinguish only one word, 'Angeliké'. Then Maroula was kissing her on both cheeks. Tears of emotion ran down the sun-lined brown face, and the thought ran through Liz's mind that Angeliké's mother might be garbed in sombre black, her face shaded by her coif, but there was warmth and kindness in her expression and a lively welcome for her daughter's friend in her brown eyes. The next minute she became aware of a young couple and two small dark-eyed boys, Angeliké's married brother and his family no doubt, she thought. Liz caught a jumble of names, but she couldn't distinguish between them. Not that it mattered, she thought, for suddenly she was surrounded by people, all obviously relatives and friends of Maroula and Petros, gathered here today to welcome the girl who brought news of Angeliké, whom they hadn't seen for many long years.

Once again Liz found herself regretting not having taken the trouble to learn something of the Greek language before coming to this country. If only she had she wouldn't feel at such a disadvantage when clearly Maroula and Petros were longing desperately for news of their daughter. 'English? Does anyone speak English?' she appealed to the crowd thronging around her, but she encountered only blank puzzled stares. Oh dear, now she would have to depend on Adam. She hadn't wanted to ask favours of him, especially seeing she had refused his offer to interpret for her, but it seemed she had no option. She turned towards him. 'Adam—' He was regarding her with his bright perceptive glance and she could swear there was a mocking light in his eyes. 'You wouldn't believe it,' she told him, 'but not one of them here can speak English. And there's so much they want to know about my friend in New Zealand.'

'Really?' He raised thick dark brows in a quizzical gesture and for a long moment she feared he was about to refuse. The next moment his dark face split into a triumphant grin. 'I thought you'd never ask!'

He broke into Greek, and although everyone was talking at once, Liz thought bewilderedly, evidently whatever it was that Adam was saying made sense, for Maroula was taking her by the arm and pointing up a stairway.

Adam's voice intruded on her thoughts. 'Maroula says she's sorry about her son being away. Seems he's gone back to America, he'll be so sorry about having missed your visit.' So that was why he wasn't here to act as interpreter, Liz reflected. She brought her mind back to Adam's tones. 'She says would you like to go to the bathroom and freshen up. I don't mind telling you I had to give her the idea for that one, but she caught on in the end.'

'Would I ever?' Liz threw him a thankful smile, then turned away to go up the twisting stairs with the Greek woman. When they reached the small room Maroula indicated the tap over a basin, and it was clear she was proud of the running water. She watched, smiling, while Liz washed her face and hands, then went to fetch a towel.

When Liz returned to the big room downstairs, all around her echoed talk and laughter. Petros, clapping his hands, at last managed to make himself heard, his strong tones rising above the clamour.

Liz flung Adam an enquiring glance. 'What now?'

'He's saying that everyone is to come to the table for wine and food. It seems it's a meal first, then present time. Let's hope,' he added in a low tone,' you've brought lots of goodies with you. It looks like there are swags of relations, Angeliké's family seem to be a fruitful lot!'

She threw him an indignant glance. 'Of course I have!'

Everyone was moving, including Petros and Maroula's two younger children, an engaging-looking boy and girl who had just come in from school. As Liz too moved towards the table she realised that Maroula at her side, was gesticulating towards the blue embroidered cloth. The next moment Liz saw with pleasure that the word 'welcome' was formed along the length of the cloth, the letters made from the bright yellow daisies that blossomed along the roadside. Liz smiled towards the Greek woman in an attempt to show her appreciation. Could it have been Angeliké who had told her mother the English word?

The volatile, laughing group crowded around the table and those who couldn't find a seat stood behind the chairs. Liz found herself seated opposite Giorgios, their guide. Despite her efforts to avoid him Petros, with much gesti-culating and a flood of Greek, was obviously insisting that Adam must sit at the side of the guest of honour. Did her hosts have the mistaken idea, she wondered, that she and Adam were a man and a woman who were in love with each other? But of course, she mused the next minute, hadn't she heard that in remote districts of Crete, the old traditions lived on and a Greek girl was never allowed to be alone with a man until the arrangement of the betrothal. Adam and herself! If only they knew, she thought wryly, and felt a knife-thrust of pain.

The crowd surged around them and she was pressed close, so close to Adam. The nearness of him, the muscular bronzed arm touching her own, was sending vibrations running through her and flinging to the winds all her resolutions that she wouldn't let herself be so tinglingly aware of him. With an effort she brought her thoughts back to her surroundings. The chatter and laughter of the volatile peasants had risen to an uproar, and plainly, she thought, this was a big day for Angeliké's parents.

As new arrivals continued to enter the room Liz wondered apprehensively if they were friends and neighbours or close relatives. For although her rucksack bulged with parcels there was a limit to the gifts she could hand out.

A worried frown creased her forehead and she glanced up to meet Adam's sardonic glance. It was an expression he seemed to keep just for her today, she mused crossly. Well, she hadn't asked him to make the trip, he had taken it on himself to come with her, she thought resentfully.

His forceful tones cut across her musing.

'Not worrying about the number of goodies you've brought with you, are you?' He had this uncanny knack of tuning in on her thoughts, damn him!

'I am a bit,' she admitted. 'There are so many—people, I mean.'

'Don't worry,' he said easily, 'most of these will be friends and neighbours of Petros and Maroula. The Cretans are a friendly lot, you might have noticed, and if they have anything to celebrate they want everyone they know to join in and share the fun. Today the whole of the village will be here. Your friend back in New Zealand will know the score and she'll have tossed in gifts for everyone, you'll see.'

Liz let out a breath of relief. 'Thank heaven for that!'

'You'd better learn the Greek word for "thank you",' he

told her drily. 'I've got a feeling you're going to need it before we leave. Can you remember "*Epharisto*"?'

'*Epharisto*,' she repeated carefully. 'Got it!'

'I'd better warn you, Cretans can be very inquisitive about folk, and devastatingly frank.'

She laughed. 'I'll leave you to cope with that! You're the language expert!'

She realised, as plate after plate was placed on the table, the long hours of preparation that must have gone to make up the varied array of Greek foods. She gazed at the great pottery bowls of salads, impressive affairs of huge tomatoes, peppers and onion, sprinkled with olives. Pilafs made of shrimps and prawns, *avgolemono*, a clear lemon-flavoured soup, boiled meat balls with rice, moussaka. There were sweets too, including honey-puffs, delicate fancies made of honey that looked to Liz like golden candyfloss, and great bowls of fresh grapes and oranges. 'Try the *tyropitta*, small cheese pies to you,' she became aware of Adam's voice, 'they're a speciality of the island.'

The food was delicious, Liz decided, and never again would she profess a dislike of Greek food. The hours in the sunlit air had sharpened her appetite and as the meal went on something of the mood of gaiety and excitement seemed to rub off on to her.

'You should try the *raki*.' Adam managed to make himself heard in a lull in the tumult of voices echoing around them.

She eyed her glass. 'Dare I? I'm sure it tastes of turpentine, but on the other hand I couldn't go back to New Zealand and confess that I hadn't really sampled the fiery spirit of Crete.'

His low forceful tone reached her through the din. '*Are* you going back, Liz?'

Enjoyment of the moment had lulled her into a state of relaxed content. 'Maybe . . . one of these days.' She held out her glass and he poured from the carafe a portion of the native wine. As the fiery spirit went down her throat she caught her breath. 'Wow! I can understand now what they say about it, that after a few glasses of *raki* you're not really with it.'

'Try this, then,' she became aware of Adam's voice, 'it's just a local wine.'

The next minute she realised that glasses were raised and heads had turned to smile in her direction. Clearly a toast was being proposed to her. She heard her own name and laughingly acknowledged the good wishes. In the ensuing clamour of voices she appealed once again to Adam. 'What's Petros saying about me?'

She was becoming accustomed to his cool mocking glance. 'Just one of their native sayings, "Be happy always".'

'Oh!' Suddenly the heartache she had all but succeeded in smothering during the last half hour, surfaced and she was swept by anguish. If only everything could be different between her and Adam, and there was nothing to part them. If only she hadn't ever discovered his real reason for liking her—correction, making a pretence of liking her. If only . . . Her eyes clouded and her soft lips drooped wistfully.

'*Smile, Liz!*' At Adam's low urgent summons she blinked and came back to the present with a start, realising that everyone was looking at her, their glasses raised.

So she flashed her brightest smile and tried to submerge herself in the happiness and goodwill that was flowing warmly around her from these kind-hearted strangers.

The wine, sweet and flavoured with almonds, relaxed her tense nerves. It was so hard, she thought on a sigh, to remember all the time how hateful and despicable Adam was, how little she really meant in his scheme of things. His kisses that had shaken her world had been no more to him than a passing interlude.

When at last the meal came to an end Liz opened her travel pack, aware of the eager faces that pressed around her. Adam had gone to join a group of Greek men at the other side of the crowded room, she could glimpse his dark head above the others, and once again she asked herself

why he had really come here with her today. The next
minute she pulled herself up sharply. Why was she thinking of him all the time anyway?

Wrenching her mind back to the present, she passed
around the photos of Angeliké and her family and then
took an attractively wrapped parcel from her pack. 'For
you, Maroula.'

Friends and relatives who were grouped around
Maroula watched with breathless interest as the Greek
woman shook out the folds of the fine linen tablecloth
exquisitely embroidered in coloured yarns, on which her
far-away daughter had spent so many hours of needle-
work. At that moment Liz knew that she had no need of
language, for Maroula's emotion-torn nut-brown face and
wet eyes said it all. Liz guessed that the cloth from New
Zealand would be far too precious a belonging to be used
for anything but an occasion of great importance such as a
family wedding.

Other gifts from Angeliké followed—jams and pre-
serves made from the produce of her adopted country,
passionfruit honey, chutney, rich and spicy, flavoured
with dark crimson tamarillos, jars of kiwi fruit, the silvery
green slices preserved in a sweet syrup.

Maroula had slipped her feet into sheepskin moccasins
she had taken from a parcel and was gazing with pride at
the huge fluffy slippers. 'You mustn't wear them in this
heat,' Liz told her, then broke off in dismay. Oh dear, she
thought, she can't understand a single word I say, and she
glanced desperately around for Adam to come to her
rescue. She was relieved to find, however, that he had
returned to her side and had overheard the words. 'Tell
her they're not to be worn in summer,' she appealed to
him, 'or the poor woman will die of heatstroke! That
they're only for wear when the snow is on the mountains.'

He grinned and interpreted the message, which for
some reason Liz failed to understand, had the effect of
sending Maroula into gales of laughter. Adam, catching
Liz's puzzled glance, sent her a conspiratorial wink. 'She
says she's not as silly as all that!'

As she took the presents one by one from her nylon pack, Liz realised how much care Angeliké had taken in choosing gifts for her loved ones in the Cretan village. There was a pipe fashioned from New Zealand timber for Petros, a bottle of kiwi fruit wine for the brother absent in America. The two younger children of the family smiled shyly as Liz fastened to the little girl's frock a gleaming paua shell brooch fashioned in the shape of a leaping dolphin, then flung a sheepskin lined jacket around the boy's small shoulders.

'Hey,' she caught Adam's prompting voice, 'sure you haven't forgotten Angeliké's sister and her husband?'

'Coming up!' Swiftly Liz dived into her pack and drew out a ring set with greenstone, the New Zealand jade. The expression of awed delight in Helene's dark eyes as she drew the ring on her finger was something she would have difficulty in describing by letter to Angeliké, Liz thought.

For Manoli there was a leather belt carved in the scrolls of a Maori design which he immediately put on, fastening the belt around his slim waist with the silver buckle.

All at once Liz became aware of wistful-eyed children who were standing at the back of the crowd. How thankful she was that her friend had included with her family presents an assortment of gifts for children and adults. 'The neighbours will be there to see you too,' Angeliké had told Liz, 'my parents will want everyone to join in the celebrations and share their happiness. No one must be left out, just hand things around to everyone. There are sweets and chocolates and cigarettes and pocket knives for the boys and bracelets for the girls.'

When all the gifts had been duly distributed, Liz had time to glance around her. Presents were being passed from hand to hand, and everyone exclaimed over the beauty or uniqueness of the wonderful nature of the gift. At least, that was how Liz interpreted the rapid gestures and excited talk of the dark-eyed women, a non-stop stream of words that appeared to be interrupted only by making the sign of the cross followed by a sigh that seemed to be a feature of this village life.

CHAPTER TEN

ALL at once the noise around them died away and through a cloud of smoke Liz saw that Giorgios, their guide, had risen to his feet. Soon, his fingers sweeping the strings of a lyre, he sang a native song, and Liz found herself struggling against the haunting sensuous melody that was taking her back to a time when she had been so wildly, foolishly happy with Adam. But of course she reminded herself as she forced her thoughts back to reality, it hadn't been the real Adam but merely a man she had dreamed up. An oh-so-wonderful male companion who was incredibly attractive, heaven to be with. A dream figure with whom for a short period she had found herself in danger of falling in love. Fortunately though, she congratulated herself, she had come to her senses in time!

Lost in her imaginings, she had scarcely realised that the song had come to an end and Petros was moving to a cleared space on the floor. Silently the crowd watched as with Cretan verve and exuberance his feet performed the intricate steps of the lively native dance. 'You mustn't applaud at the end,' Adam whispered to her, 'he's dancing for his own satisfaction, not for anyone else.'

Soon everyone was dancing, arms linked to form an open circle. As always Adam's touch as he threw his arm around her shoulders, electrified her. As she moved to the wildly accelerated rhythm she was caught up in the exhilaration around her, and everything slipped away from mind but the excitement of the moment and the sensuous beat of the singing lyre and bouzouki.

It must be the wine, she told herself in a pause in the rhythmic beat, that was making her forget everything else but the pleasure of the evening. Blame the music too, she told herself, the atmosphere, the feeling of being in a faraway world remote from everyday living. In this state of relaxation she couldn't continue to be unpleasant to anyone, not even to Adam. Somehow tonight she was finding it very difficult to hate Adam.

As the night wore on the music became louder, the room thick with pipe and cigarette smoke. Dark aquiline faces streamed with sweat as the music went faster and faster until the floor boards creaked with the stamping feet of Crete dancers. During pauses in the dancing there was wine, the clinking of glasses, the murmured sound of '*hyrrs*'. Liz lost count of time until she chanced to glance down at the watch on Adam's tanned wrist. Tonight he never seemed to be far from her side. Maybe, she mused, he was taking his position as interpreter seriously. Aloud she said in surprise, 'Heavens, I had no idea it was so late. The night's almost over. Why didn't you tell me?'

He raised thick dark brows. 'And ruin everyone's pleasure?'

A little later, however, as guests began to move towards Petros and Maroula, Liz had no need of language to realise that the party was coming to an end. As neighbours and friends made their warm and affectionate farewells, she gathered together the gifts that these generous people had given her—a hand-loomed wall hanging woven in a traditional design, freshly gathered black cherries fashioned into a bouquet, a jar of honey and a bunch of red roses already wilting in the heat of the crowded room. When she had placed the gifts in her pack she realised that she and Adam were the centre of a laughing group. Swarthy faces were pressing around them, their voices raised in words that were repated over and over again. Clearly, Liz thought, whatever the meaning of the phrase it was a matter that demanded an answer, and something that concerned both her and Adam. She threw him a curious glance.

'I don't know what they're on about. Do you?'

Through the tumult of voices she caught his low murmur. 'Sure I know.'

'You might let me in on it,' she taunted.

'Sure you want to know?' There was a curl at the corners of his well-shaped lips. 'I warn you, Liz, you mightn't like it.'

She laughed. 'Try me!'

'Right! You've asked for it! It seems,' he said softly, 'that they're mighty curious about the date we've set for the wedding.'

'W-wedding?' she gasped. The next moment she tried to cover her confusion by saying quickly, 'Whatever could have given them that idea—No, don't tell me!' For all at once there had flashed back to her mind a recollection of Adam explaining to her the significance of a visit of a Cretan girl, accompanied by a man friend, to friends and relatives. To these mountain peasants such a visit could have but one meaning—a betrothal.

The wine, the heat of the crowded room, was making her feel slightly muzzy and far, far too relaxed. All she could come up with was: 'That must have been a hard one to answer!'

'Not really, I told them the truth.' His low vibrant tones were threaded with a note she couldn't fathom. 'That it all depends on you.'

She raised blue-grey eyes clouded with bewilderment to his face and then it happened. The wild excitement pulsing through her, the surge of happiness, drawing her to him in spite of herself. A feeling of delicious lassitude making her sway slightly towards him. Adam . . . his dark hair in disorder from the dancing, eyes alight with a message that was unmistakable: 'I love you.' The next minute she jerked herself back to sanity. 'It's the wine, the fiery Cretan *raki*, that's making him look at me like that, causing me to feel this way about him.' Through the confusion flooding through her she gathered together her rioting senses. She even managed to infuse a careless note into her voice. 'So that was why they were all looking at me?'

She turned away and the next minute Angeliké's family

were crowding close, taking her hands in their warm grasp and planting affectionate kisses on both cheeks.

The group accompanied her and Adam out into the clear night air where Giorgios was waiting with the donkeys, dark shapes outlined against a silvered scene. The moon was a polished silver disc in the clear night sky, and as she looked at the mountain crags rising above Liz was thankful she wasn't making the journey alone, for a guide wouldn't be anyone to talk to. But with Adam riding beside her—There she went once more, she chided herself, thinking of Adam, halfway to liking him all over again despite all she knew of him.

Their new friends left them where the village lane changed into a goat track winding down dark slopes and Liz threw kisses back over her shoulder as they moved away on a gale of laughter and good wishes.

Presently as they took a track winding down to a rocky gorge she asked herself. 'Is this really happening?' The clip-clop of the donkeys' hooves on the stony surface sounded loud in the stillness of the Cretan night, the crags high above black against the moon, had the eerie look of a dream scene, the Cretan youth talking in a language she didn't understand, and Adam . . .

Oddly, the journey that had seemed so long earlier in the day now seemed to Liz to be all too short a trip, and they rode into the silent village before she realised they were so close to civilization. Adam's red car was the only vehicle in sight and when they reached it she slipped down from her mount to the cobbles of the street. Something warned her that it would be better for her peace of mind not to risk Adam's help when dismounting from her wooden saddle, not when it meant the dangerous rapture of being held close in his arms.

She waited while Adam paid the Cretan youth, then Giorgios waved them farewell and led the donkeys away. Adam flung open the car door for Liz and she slipped into the passenger seat.

As they took the dark road winding down a slope her

thoughts were busy. On this journey through the night alone together, maybe he would take the opportunity of trying to heal the breach between them? He might imagine that the attraction he held for her—why not admit it?—had been strong enough tonight to make her forget all about her sense of betrayal and her determination to resist any efforts on his part to get around her for purposes of his own. She steeled herself in readiness for any such attempts on his part, somehow she'd got to make herself strong and determined enough to resist his masculine charisma. But she need not have bothered, she told herself a little later as they sped on, because Adam made little attempt at conversation. He was seemingly intent on driving at speed as they hurtled up dark slopes and swung around hairpin bends.

Liz clutched at the dashboard as they swung around a sharp bend in the mountain road. Trying to make her voice ultra-calm, she commented, 'You're in a big hurry tonight,' and couldn't resist adding, 'Anyone would think you couldn't wait to get rid of me!'

'Not scared, are you?' He threw her a sideways glance, and she found herself wishing she could see the expression of his eyes.

'Not with you,' she said, and could have bitten out her tongue at the admission that had slipped from her lips.

For despite the speed at which they were moving, she felt entirely confident with Adam. There was something about him. You had the feeling that if he cared for a girl—She brought her thoughts up with a jolt. There she went again, romancing, dreaming, and about Adam of all men. Adam who had betrayed her trust once and would probably do it again if he got the chance. But he wouldn't, not now that she was forewarned.

She should be glad, she told herself on a sigh, that he was no longer interested in her. Clearly she had at last got through to him that she was a girl who knew her own mind and when she said 'no sale' she stuck to her decision. But what a waste, on a night like this! If only Adam was as she had at first imagined him, he would be the one man in the world for her. Now where, she asked herself the next moment, had that absurd thought come from?

Her thoughts wandered and she wondered bleakly if he too were regretting the waste of this journey on a black and silver night, wishing he was with his woman friend Karen who was sophisticated and mature and whom, he loved, really loved.

And yet somehow she gained the impression that he was angry, that the speed at which they were hurtling through the night was his way of letting off steam. Because of his inner frustrations concerning herself? She thrust the supposition aside as ridiculous. He couldn't really care about her, it had been only pretence—enough to take her in, but it had been acting just the same. Well, she stared ahead at the headlamps playing over the dusty road, if he wanted to play it that way it suited her fine. She didn't attempt to make conversation and they went the rest of the way in a heavy silence.

When at length they drew up outside the hotel, Adam turned to her, unsmiling. 'I'll see you to the villa.'

She knew it was useless to argue the matter, so she hurried along, trying to keep up with his long strides, as they took the narrow goat track together. In the moonshine she stumbled over a tree root embedded in the path and swiftly he took her hand. As always his touch sent the blood racing through her veins.

'It's all right,' she snatched her hand from his grasp. Don't touch me, please, Adam, she implored silently. She was all too well aware of the heady magic of his touch and tonight, she told herself over her whirling senses, she must keep her wits about her and concentrate on the really important things like his using her to further his business affairs and his lovemaking being just a trick. A trick that for her could have serious consequences if she didn't watch herself.

When they reached the courtyard they paused and her heart was beating fast. Adam together with the moon-silvered scene made a combination hard to resist and she knew this was the moment when she should leave him quickly, a no-fuse moment, yet still she lingered.

'Goodnight, Liz.' She caught the tense note in his voice. She looked up at him. 'Thanks . . . for everything. I couldn't have got there today but for you.'

All at once his tone was soft and deep, the tone that did things to her heart. 'Why don't you thank me properly?'

Caught in a spell, she made no move to avoid him and the next moment she was in his arms, enfolded close to him. He said huskily, 'Shall I be seeing you again, Liz?'

'No, no—I don't know,' she whispered in confusion.

'I could help you to make up your mind.' His low voice started the trembling in her. 'Why are you trembling, Liz?' Then his seeking lips found hers and she was carried away to a world of ecstasy by the heady rapture of his kiss. At last he released her and she caught his deep exultant chuckle. 'I knew I could persuade you—*my way*!'

Slowly, slowly, through a daze of happiness, Liz came back to reality. There was something she should remember. Then memories came rushing back and she wrenched herself free, pushing the dark hair back from her forehead in a nervous gesture. 'You'll never persuade me to change my mind.' She was breathing hard. 'That really would solve your problem, wouldn't it?' she flung at him. The moment the words were out she longed to call them back. But he had asked for them, hadn't he?

'So long as we understand each other!' The angry words flicked her raw nerves like a whip. The next moment he had left her.

And it was all her own fault! The sickening thought was like cold steel passing through her. But she had to fling those bitter words at him, she'd had to, for tonight his smooth technique to 'soften up Liz' had worked all too successfully. She put her hands to her burning cheeks, struck with the humiliating remembrance of how eagerly she had responded to his caress.

Blindly she stumbled towards the door and let herself

into the house. Moving to the window, she glimpsed in the first flush of dawn, a masculine figure striding up the slope, then she couldn't see him for the tears that blinded her eyes. She should be pleased, she told herself bleakly, that she had kept her resolve not to be taken in all over again by his touch that could send her world spinning out of orbit. But she felt only this ache of longing. Adam had gone away, she swallowed over the lump in her throat, and this time it was for ever.

A little later she decided that in this restless state, it would be impossible for her to sleep. She might just as well work in the taverna where physical toil might help to deaden this anguish and the heavy sense of loss.

Fortunately, she found as she took her place behind the counter of the seaside café, it was one of the days when the tour buses pulled in and everyone was kept frantically busy coping with the good-tempered holiday crowd. Even Nikos was helping, often pausing in his task of collecting coffee mugs from tables to burst into one of his lively native songs, to the delight of the customers. They were so helpful, Xenia and Nikos, and if business continued in this manner soon she would have no financial worries. She should be so happy, it was what she'd wanted, wasn't it? And yet . . .

Doggedly she went on with her tasks, even, in a brief pause in counter work, deciding to clean out a high cupboard that she hadn't yet opened. She was standing on a stool, tossing out old newspapers, when a piece of paper that was fluttering through the air caught her attention. She jumped down to the tiled floor, her gaze scanning the delivery note that the carriers who had delivered the equipment must have thrust into the high cupboard for safe keeping. But something was wrong. She felt emotion engulfing her, making her feel confused and lightheaded. For this document was made out by a firm in Heraklion for goods to be delivered to the taverna on the beach and charged to Adam's account.

Adam! A trembling seized her and as from a distance

she became aware of Xenia's face, the dark eyes concerned as she tried by means of pantomime to persuade Liz to sit down.

It's just not possible! It doesn't make any sense! The conflicting thoughts tumbled wildly through her distraught mind. Not Adam! Because why would he do such a thing? But he had and that must mean that the action was to his advantage, though she couldn't imagine in what way. Dazedly she took the mug of hot coffee Xenia was handing to her. The Greek woman must be wondering why Liz, who was usually bursting with energy, was now acting so strangely. But no doubt, she reflected, Xenia would put her odd behaviour down to the all-night party in the mountain village—and the fiery *raki*!

Throughout the remainder of the day Liz moved like a girl in a dream. She supposed her hands must have performed their conventional tasks and her lips must have smiled a welcome to customers just as usual, because no one appeared to notice anything untoward in her behaviour. Except Xenia, who continued to regard Liz with friendly concern. If only she could explain to the friendly Greek woman that there was nothing wrong with her health!

In her mind she went over and over the reason for Adam having purchased the goods on her behalf, his strange secrecy in the matter. A wave of humiliation washed over her. How he must have grinned to himself at the glib explanation she had confided to him, her naïve assumption of Kostas' change of heart due to his fear of scandal. She couldn't *wait* until the end of the day when she could go to the hotel and face Adam, let him know in no uncertain terms that she knew all about his sneaky action and she wanted an explanation from him.

It was the longest day that she had ever known, but at last she said goodbye to Nikos and Xenia and hurried up to the villa.

'One thing's for sure,' she mused wryly as she glanced towards her mirror in the bedroom, 'Adam won't think

I've come to see him to make things up between us, to tell him I didn't mean all those horrible things I said to him last night. Not with this ghastly white face and those awful blue shadows under my eyes.' But he wouldn't care one bit what she looked like. Unconsciously she sighed. She wasn't the woman he was interested in, so what did it matter?

Caught up as she was in her own problems and the questions to which there seemed no answers, it wasn't until she neared the imposing entrance of the high white building that it occurred to her that Adam might not be available tonight. 'He'd better be in, 'she thought grimly, 'I can't bear this suspense for much longer,' and found herself looking directly into his face as he stepped from his car.

'Liz!' Something leaped in his eyes, twin shafts of pure pleasure. Surely she must have been mistaken, she told herself the next moment. No man could admire a girl who looked the way she did at this moment, especially not Adam, who didn't *really* care. Aloud she said breathlessly, 'I had to see you! It's something important! Something I just can't understand!'

'You look all in.' His eyes were dark with compassion. 'Come along inside and I'll get you a stiff whisky—'

She shook her head. 'No, no—'

'Let me take you for a drive, then,' he offered gently.

'If you like.' Dazedly she let him see her into the passenger seat of the red car.

For a moment he hesitated, his hand resting on the starting key. 'What's the trouble, Liz? You can tell me.'

'You!' She felt a wild urge towards hysteria.

He made no comment but started the engine and soon they were taking a white dusty road winding up a steep slope. 'It's a bit more private than the Hermes, the spot I'm taking you to, and the view from the top of the cliff is out of this world.'

All at once she was feeling unutterably weary. 'Anywhere will do, it doesn't matter to me.' Leaning back in her seat, she closed her eyes, and when she opened them again he was braking to a stop on a high point overlooking a sea that was flooded with the shimmering golden pathway of the setting sun.

He turned to face her. 'Come on, Liz, tell me, what's all this about? What's the problem?'

It's strange, the thought shot through her mind, but he seems determined to overlook last night and the bitter words I threw at him. Aloud she said accusingly, 'It's you!'

He grinned. 'That's all right, then, we can sort it out between us.'

'Can we?' She raised clear grey-blue eyes to his steadfast gaze. 'Why didn't you tell me,' she said very low, 'that it was you who paid for all the goods I needed for the taverna and had all the stuff delivered there? It was you all the time! I only found out about it today when I happened to come across a printed docket from the firm who sold the goods, with your name on it. It was hidden away in a high cupboard that I've never used.

'Someone must have slipped up there, by the sound of it,' he said easily, 'but I guess you were bound to find out about it sooner or later.'

'But what I can't understand,' she pursued, 'is why you didn't let on to me about it at the time?'

'Why?' An enigmatic smile played around his lips. 'Come on, Liz, be honest with me. Would you have taken it from me, do you think?'

'No, I wouldn't!' she acknowledged quickly, and added on a sigh, 'but I guess that was because I couldn't ever trust you. I still can't believe you would go to all that trouble and expense just for me.' She raised her heavy gaze to his face. 'Why did you?'

'Just,' lifting her hand in his, he pressed her fingers to his lips, 'that you seemed to be in need of a helping hand to get that project of yours off the ground.'

'But—but—' Her heart was thudding wildly and she tried to pin down the thoughts that were rushing through her mind. 'It wouldn't do you any good. That way you'd never get the property you want so much.'

He said gravely, his eyes never leaving hers, 'I wasn't thinking of business deals, Liz, I was thinking of you.' Once again he pressed her fingers to his lips. 'I'm always thinking of you, I can't seem to get you out of my mind.' His voice was low with emotion, 'I love you, it's as simple as that.'

The unexpectedness of his words stunned her. Was this too part of the makebelieve? All at once it seemed very important that she be sure. Forcing down the wild excitement that threatened to engulf her, she murmured, 'Karen—'

'*Karen!*' He bent on her his incredulous stare. 'You're not telling me that you thought—Good grief, she's my sister! If that's what you were thinking all this time—'

Suddenly fire was pulsing through her senses. She wasn't tired any more but gloriously, wonderfully happy!

'Why waste time in thinking anyway?' With infinite tenderness he ran his hands down her pale cheeks. 'Tell me you love me.' She barely caught the low tone, ragged with emotion.

'I've always loved you, right from the start!' The truth burst on her mind with a wild sense of elation. 'Only I wouldn't let myself believe—' The words were lost as he gathered her close and his seeking lips found hers. Without her volition her arms crept up to link themselves around his neck and her fingers curled around the soft dark hair she had always longed to touch. Then the world slipped out of focus and there was only ecstasy and a deep sense of belonging.

Adam released her at last, to gaze down into her flushed, tremulous face. 'My darling,' his voice was unsteady, 'no more problems—'

Her eyes were glinting with a teasing light. 'Only one! I've just remembered about Katina and her dowry.'

'Oh, that's all taken care of now,' the words were

punctuated with kisses, 'comes under the heading of project number two—remember?'

'Oh yes,' she nestled close in his arms, 'the scheme that was guaranteed to get you what you wanted? I can't imagine what you had in mind?'

'Can't you?' he whispered against her lips. 'It's a man-and-woman thing. I want you to be my wife. My darling,' his low tones were husky with emotion, 'say you will!' Her warm response to the urgency of his lips left no doubt as to her answer.